TALES
FROM
THE
TEXAS
WOODS

M I C H A E L
MOORCOCK

TALES
FROM
THE
TEXAS
WOODS

AUSTIN, TEXAS

P.O. Box 140005
Austin, Texas 78714
fax 512-858-7282
www.mojo.com

For all my Texas pards --

Rick, Ben, Joe,
Bruce, Mary, Charlie,
John, Jan, Bill, Neill, Lyn, Davis,
my friends at the Opera House,
the boys down at the Oyster Bar

*-- and to the memory of
my friend Leigh Brackett,
who added so substantially
to the authentic romance of the West.*

Are we fodder for
our fish to feed upon?

— Lobkowitz,
Sailing Days

CONTENTS

INTRODUCTION

Dear Reader,

The first encounter with the West that I recall with any real clarity was watching Gary Cooper, a dandified *Plainsman*, featured on a program with an equally dashing Joel McCrea. *Buffalo Bill* had been shot in old-fashioned Technicolor and captured exactly the quality of the Western annuals, with titles like *Scouts in Buckskin* and *Heroes of the Prairie*, that I inherited from my father and grandfather.

These large books, often deluxe versions of weekly boys' magazines, contained wonderful coloured plates by people like Stanley L. Wood and retailed the adventures of various frontier gentlemen adventurers — knights of the prairie whose origins were primarily in Fenimore Cooper and American dime novels written by people like Ned Buntline and Colonel Prentiss Ingraham. Buffalo Bill, Kit Carson, Texas Jack and many others were all familiar names to me as soon as I could read. While the V-2 rockets fell outside, I used my fallen horse for cover and tried to judge how many Indians I had to fight before I could get to the fort and warn of danger...

I think the working cowboy came to my attention first in the stories of Clarence E. Mulford, whose novels I read for the same reason I read Edgar Rice Burroughs and George Bernard Shaw — they were the only books in the house. I found Mulford novels, with their emphasis on ranch life and the actual work of the cowboy, more interesting than the likes of Louis L'Amour who had, for my taste, already become genre-bound and too formalised.

I would say the modern screen westerner first attracted me when Tom Mix took his Cowboy Show to Europe and was instrumental in rescuing Mickey Rooney, boy-king of a Ruritanian state, in one of the most spectacular and enjoyable bits of genre-blending I've ever had the pleasure of watching. I talk about *My Pal, The King* elsewhere.

By the time I was sixteen I was earning a living writing short stories, many of which were fantasy, some of which were jungle tales. Many others were westerns. I had a character called Johnny Lonesome and I also wrote about Buck Jones, Kit Carson and Buffalo Bill, who appeared in monthly pocket-size books called *Cowboy Picture Library*, whose companion titles in *Thriller Picture Library* including Robin Hood, Billy the Kid and Dick Turpin.

Buck Jones remained a living legend and a hero in England long after he died a true hero's death at Boston's Coconut Grove in 1942. In fact, when I first started writing the stories I had no idea that Jones was a real person.

At the age of seventeen, sitting in a dark little room in South London in the late 1950's, I earned a wonderful living writing about an Arizona I'd never visited, about the Apache and the Comanche, about the torments of the Texas weather. I retailed bits of prairie lore to boys who had as much direct experience of Western life as I had. We were part of a general zeitgeist already changing attitudes towards the Indian and we believed we were depicting a culture realistically, even if it was actually as romanticised and sentimentalised as *Dances With Wolves*.

As soon as I could, I headed for the West and South West. No American tourist making a beeline for an equally romanticised Windsor Castle or Whitechapel ever felt a thrill as great as mine when I saw my first butte. And it didn't feel bad giving lifts to hitch-hiking Navajos, either, even if their conversation was proverbially clipped. It was all far better than I had hoped to find. And I consoled myself that while I had written about places and peoples I'd never encountered until now, I was actually here and it wasn't too different. I'd discovered that my fiction was at least a fading echo of the actuality but probably owed as much to the great Max Brand. He produced most of *his* best Westerns from a fourteenth century Italian villa, turning them out a speed which made my pace seem positively stately.

One thing I've learned from my travels is that the wonders of the world are always better in reality than you can possibly imagine. The reality of the Sinai desert makes the best scenes in *Lawrence of Arabia* seem positively lacklustre. And so it was when I first saw the sun setting over the Rocky Mountains. We were high up, above the clouds, in a little mining town hovering on the edge of oblivion (and probably these days surviving as a tourist village), when that mighty wash of colour began to flood across the snowy Colorado peaks.

Spectacular enough to make me gasp, the view had the quality Coleridge described when he was first introduced by Wordsworth to the English Lakes. I had not believed the colours could be so rich and vivid. Tears came to my eyes. Here were exactly the wild shades and burning swathes of colour, the equivalent of the sensational fiction I had read, which I had honestly accepted as examples of the printer's exaggeration rather than representations of reality! The clearness of the air increased the contrasts. The waves of subtle colour poured over the slopes and ridges of the mountains. They stained the weather-battered timber of the false fronts, the saloons which still used Yankee names, like *The Pennsylvania Grill*, to look classy and had yet to retitle their establishments *The Golden Nugget* or *The Buckin' Bronc* to fulfill tourist expectations. Here was awesome Nature just as described by all those early American romantics I had enjoyed so thoroughly and had believed half-crazed.

Crazed they might have been, swigging laudanum and swinging their mocassins over the edge of the Great Divide, but they hadn't exaggerated. They had done their best and, like me, they'd hardly come close. So much of the American West, no matter how urbanised or sanitised, retains that same raw, vibrant quality which tells you Nature still hasn't given up the fight — has scarcely lost a skirmish. The Texas Hill Country, geologically sharing much in common with the Sussex downs, might provide scenes straight from Constable — shady ponds and tranquil cows — but Southern England lacks the scorpions, rattlers and copperheads, not to mention all the other ill-tempered flying, crawling and pouncing livestock which still snarls and lurks in the woods around our old Texas house and occasionally pays us a visit. Hurricanes, tornadoes and floods are also rather more frequent and serious threats than we knew in Oxfordshire.

The *Buffalo Bill Annuals* and the Zane Grey novels never really told you how profoundly uncivilised so much of the West, especially the South West, remains, how easy it is to understand that we are pretty puny and vulnerable creatures in comparison to the vast natural forces which materially control our lives and our destinies.

INTRODUCTION

The likes of McMurtry or McCarthy probably come closest, in their exaggerated riffs on genre, to giving that sense of the savagery and fragility of human existence, that threat of violent, sudden death many Westerners still cherish as creating the state of mind which made their ancestors strong, life-loving, independent and profoundly courteous.

The reality isn't Buck Jones' Hollywood West or even Kit Carson's legendary West, but the romance is authentic. It is rooted in the ancient landscapes and histories of this vast, astonishing, mysterious territory. It is rooted in some of the most stunning natural beauty in the world. It is rooted deep in powerful individual experience, in vivid reality. That's why the Romance of the West continues to fascinate and engage us, why writers are constantly inspired and replenished by it. I believe it's also why we have to protect that physical and psychic territory from exploitation, simplification, sentimentality and sanitization. It represents a principle far more important to our survival than any tacit support we might continue to give, through our ballot boxes, to the voracious rich.

Michael Moorcock
Lost Pines
Texas

N EWS CAME to the young vigilante that the White Dogs were on the warpath again. What had caused the Apache Nation's most bloodthirsty mystical sect to revive their vendetta against the Texans — and where had so many warriors come from?? And why had they kidnapped Tex Brady's beautiful young wife? The Masked Buckaroo intended to find out — even if it meant chasing some fanatical religious fundamentalists to the gates of Hell — and beyond!!

THE GHOST WARRIORS
A previously unpublished story of
THE MASKED BUCKAROO

by Warwick Colvin Jr.
Author of 'A Texan Revenge',
'Tex Brady's Secret',
'Tex of the Circle Squared',
'The Masked Buckaroo's Courtship',
'Dealin' Straight', 'Turnin' Trails',
'Herdin' Days', 'Talkin' Nights',
'Fryin' Frogs', 'Ridin' Point',
'Birthin' Beeves', 'Ropin' Broncs',
'Buckin' Bulls' , 'Eatin' Lead',
'Suckin' Emus', 'Smokin' Weed,
'Shovelin' Chips', 'Raisin' Roses',
'Windy's Last Yodel', 'Tex's Daughters',
'Range War Holiday',
'Scrapin' Barrels' &c. &c.

7

For Clarence E. Mulford

Chapter One
El Lobo Blanco

SHORTY, PINTO PETE, The Breed Papoose, and some of the other hands were up on the West Range pretending to mend fences and find strays but actually, as their boss was aware, searching out shade and sweet water because the heat was so hard and dry it felt like a sack of old cement on your sweat-soaked back and the real reason Tex, head wrangler and owner of the outfit, had sent them up there was to keep some kind of look out, which was just as well because Shorty squints up from where he's standing neck high in a pool of mud and shades his eyes and says to his dozing compadres, "Ain't that Swedish Charlie makin' dust yonder?"

Shorty was the binoculars of the Circle Squared Ranch on account of his extreme long-sightedness, so it was a while before his identification was confirmed. It was indeed, the rest agreed, Swedish Charlie, sometimes known as 'Sarajevo', who was riding in as if he'd eaten ten bowls of chili and was about to soil his breeches. He was standing in his stirrup when he reached us and brought his pony to a spectacular 'Mexican skid' so that he was on the ground before his mount knew she had stopped galloping.

He was all dust. His eyes shone out of the dirt like frightened diamonds and it only took him two words to explain his condition.

"*El Lobo*," he said and pointed behind him. He went off to relieve himself against a yucca while Shorty and the others saddled up and checked their Winchesters.

"Damn," said Shorty, cinching himself into his gear and wishing he'd paid more attention to his weapons when he should have. "I thought that sucker was supposed to be six feet under!" He took his Peacemaker from its battered holster and tried to spin the chamber. "Oh, god damn!" From one compartment he dug out a disgusting mixture of oil and hair. The gun was no better for his attention. He put it away, relying as usual on his rifle.

"I've been sayin' about that pistol," said Grumpy with deep satisfaction, swinging up alongside him.

"You've been sayin' 'I told you so' all your life, Grumpy," said the Breed Papoose, squinting his handsome eyes to show he spoke in fun. "I'm lookin' forward to the day I take an arrow or a bullet an' find your ugly mug leanin' over me to tell me how I should've seen it comin'." And he patted his own holster. "An' when it happens, Grumpy, don't say I didn't warn ya'..."

Emphatically he turned down the brim of his wide Mexican sombrero and kicked his pony forward, whistling *The Streets of Laredo* in that ostentatious, elaborate way of his.

Over his shoulder Charlie told them that at least one war party of Apache, employing their usual clever strategies, were maybe twenty miles off but moving in fast. They had torn up tramway and cut telegraph wires. He had seen two other distant war-bands and heard of more — though they could be reports of the same parties.

If their leader wasn't *El Lobo Blanco* he had certainly convinced the Indians that he was.

One thing was certain — they were coming together and their War Chief bore the Black Lance, the lost totem, their legendary symbol of redemption and revenge. Following this potent weapon, which was also their *ginam*, nothing less than an Apache army was on its way. News was that they'd already taken and gutted the Pecos Express and destroyed the tramway as far as De Quincey, making it impossible for the army to bring up troops quickly.

Charlie said that the general wisdom was that the White Dogs were on the war-path again. Word was *El Lobo Blanco* had returned from the dead and was leading them. He had been the most feared Apache on the border. Cunning, clever and almost supernaturally lucky he had nearly destroyed the Circle Squared once before. The boys left Grumpy, Windy O'Day and Swedish Charlie to follow as rearguard and took off like bullets for the relative security of the Brady Ranch.

The big sprawling fortified house and its various outbuildings were arranged around a good, deep well. The ranch was capable of withstanding for months anything but overwhelming numbers. Its situation, on a lush plain, gave it every advantage and it could not be taken by surprise. Tex Brady's father had built the place in the years when Indian raids were common and there was no cavalry station nearby to make a savage think twice.

Here, single-handedly, he had defended his cabin while his wife gave birth to his son and half the Apache nation seemed to descend on them as if some instinct told the Coaxinca, the Merengo, the Kakatanawa and the Chirichaua that a great warrior was being born to the whites — a warrior who, if he survived, would become their noblest and most admired adversary! They seemed determined that he should not survive.

11

But survive he did — and grew to young manhood at Dulwich College in England — until recalled hastily to Texas with the news that his father was murdered and the Circle Squared Ranch possessed by Mr Paul Minct, the notorious land-grabber. That tale of vengeance, redemption and love has been told already.

Now the boys skidded into the compound and dismounted in a storm of dust, their chaps flapping about their legs as they ran towards the big house just as Jenny Brady, Tex's beautiful and very recent bride, and Don Lorenzo, his grey-haired old mentor, came out onto the porch.

Shorty wasted no time conveying to his mistress and her friend what Swedish Charlie had conveyed to him.

Jenny and Don Lorenzo immediately sprang into action. Barricades were raised, rifle-slits were tested, ammunition was brought out and the two Gatling guns mounted on their swivels, covering the greater part of the surrounding range while a rider was sent to Los Pinos to warn the citizens and bring the boss back.

T EX WAS HELPING out at the circuit court where his friend, the 'Prairie Green Incorruptible', Judge Abraham Peakiss, was dispensing that even-handed law which had made him the most respected authority from Galveston to Port Sabatini.

When Shorty found Tex he was about to enjoy an evening drink in the Gin-U-Wine Oyster Bar just down the street from the old French court-house. The judge was with him and so was one of the plaintiffs the judge had just fined, shaking him by the hand, buying everybody a drink and thanking the old man for his verdict.

Swiftly the foreman blurted out the news. Nobody asked him to repeat himself. Judge Peakiss hurried off to send some telegrams. Captain Gideon went to order an express rider to Austin, requesting urgent reinforcements. Mayor Borden called a general town meeting. Lizzy La Paine demanded someone's protection, preferably Tex's. Sheriff Omar Hunt was at the MacGregor farm delivering the usual writ. The plaintiff goggled, turned pale and seemed to be looking around for something to kill himself with. *El Lobo* had that kind of credibility.

Tex Brady ran to his hotel, grabbed up his simple kit and followed Shorty to the ostlers, where his great-hearted mare Brenda was already saddled and waiting. As always, she was eager to be off. Her ancestors had borne the chivalry of Arabia and galloped with the British at Alhambra, Bengazi and Wadi-al-Djinn. Toledo steel was in her bones. Marekshi powder was in her blood.

Soon the two cowboys were riding hell for leather across the open prairie. The only difference was that now Tex Brady wore the famous blue and red outfit with the black mask and white sombrero of his *alter ego* — the legendary Masked Buckaroo! His reason for donning the costume was his reputation amongst all Indians as an honest broker. It might be the edge which saved their lives. Everyone respected the Masked Buckaroo.

Following the glinting track of the military tramway which had opened up the wild Texas frontier to civilization, they used neither quirts nor spurs, simply calm, encouraging words, to maintain that wild pace. There was not a motor — steam or electric — to match them in their own element where man and mount became the same creature, thinking and acting as one. Tex's father had always maintained that justice and kindness made simple economic sense. "You get more out of an animal and more out of an Indian if you treat 'em with respect."

A stern disciplinarian and a great patriarch, that old Cattle Baron thought cruelty made no sense at all. He had co-existed with the Indians by acknowledging their ancient rights and customs, for which they were perfectly prepared to allow him some modern rights and customs.

He had no romantic notions about the kind of people they were. They saw their fundamental survival to be dependent upon their military ascendancy, their reputation as vicious conquerors. They had been practising tribal genocide as a way of life since time began.

He knew that a balance of power existed and that if he was ever at a disadvantage, depending upon their prevailing mood and practical needs, they would finish him and everyone else on his ranch. They assumed the same of him without understanding that he believed alternatives to be available.

Like the Indians, he was acting from what he took for profound moral imperatives. He did not know how much invisible power he derived, in Indian eyes, from those people in Washington he so despised. For the times, however, his views were enlightened. Behind his back, because they dared say nothing to his terrible, battle-scarred face, the other ranchers and towners had called Meredith Brady an Indian-lover.

The mystical Secret Society of the Kakatanawa Apache known as the White Dog Circle had tested his sentiments. It was one of those cults which catches on and spreads from tribe to tribe faster than slurry through a swimming-hole.

A desperate substitute for real power, maybe, but it causes a lot of trouble while it's running. The chief shaman of the White Dogs was a Kiowa Apache trouble-maker called Ulrucha-na-o, which means 'Pale Wolf' in his dialect. They believed that, as a presentiment of his coming death, a warrior saw a pale wolf following him. However, if the wolf ran ahead of him, that meant his life ran on, also. So long as he continued to follow the wolf. It was a good way of keeping your followers in line.

Pale Wolf's charismatic personality as much as his religious pros-
elytizing drew in bored young braves with no future and a history of
defeat who believed it might be possible to drive back the whites
with magic and drugs as well as courage. When Ulrucha gave the
word and lifted up the Black Lance they were ready to go on the
war-path confident in the understanding that they were protected
by powerful magic and that their weapons were equally charmed.

This made them even braver and their attacks all the fiercer. And
it carried the luck of the devil. For eight months they did seem to
lead charmed lives, running roughshod over Texas in one last, long,
cruel, spiritually-enhancing blood-letting. This seems common to
the generality of religions, whose adherents justify the most elaborate horrors and torments in the promotion and establishment of
their faith.

No-one called Colonel Meredith Brady an Indian-lover after he
had led the war against Ulrucha and his White Dog Ghost Soldiers.
The final battle between him and the fighting shaman was a proud
legend amongst both peoples. Suffice to say, Ulrucha's scalp was
brought back to his enemy's lodge.

How Brady's son made reconciliation with the Kakatanawa
Apache and became their blood-brother is another story. Tex had
learned a great deal about Apache torture and tactics and had gained
several kinds of respect for the Indians. When the affair was con-
cluded, Tex had thought there could never be war between Apache
and Texan again. Yet here was the worst news possible!

Hours later, after some tense moments and faster than seemed
physically possible, the two men reached the compound of the Circle
Squared and threw themselves off their exhausted ponies, calling for
hot water and fresh ammunition.

After a few moments they noted the eery silence of the ranch.
Though it was evening, no lamps had been lit. From somewhere

15

came the noises of chickens and hogs, the whicker of a horse, perhaps the sound of a hammer rising and falling, but no human voices greeted them.

It was then that Shorty wordlessly pointed out the still, dark shape on the porch. It was the body of a black retriever. It had been shot through the eye with a white-fletched Kakatanawa Apache arrow.

"You ever seen that dog before, Shorty?" murmured Tex, putting fingers to the creature's throat.

"Nope," says Shorty. "Looks like a man's good hound dog, though."

A sharp sound from somewhere inside.

Tex Brady grew instantly alert, his hands falling onto the pearl handles of his twin revolvers.

"There's something funny going on here, Shorty," he gritted. "And I have to admit I don't like the smell of it..."

Chapter Two

The Scent of the Wolf

A S THE TWO men listened, the slow, regular hammering continued. It was coming from the bunk house. Their guns in their fists, the young cowboys approached the big building cautiously, kicking open the doors and ducking quickly into the shadows. The noise was soon identified.

In the middle of the common room, tied to chairs which had in turn been placed on the old oaken table at the center, were Grumpy, Pinto Pete, Windy O'Day, Swedish Charlie and The Breed Papoose. They were wearing nothing but their pink union suits, boots and hats. They were gagged. Some of the other boys were equally discommoded, lying in corners of the room. It had been The Breed Papoose who had made the noise, rapping on the table with his fancy silver boot heels.

"Somehow," said The Masked Buckaroo as his Bowie knife expertly sliced through rope and cloth, "this has none of the earmarks of an Apache raid."

"What about the arrow?" Shorty said. "That looks and smells right."

But Tex said nothing, merely frowning as he thought the problem over.

He would make no judgements until he had heard the boys out.

WINDY O'DAY, TEX'S oldest sidekick and confidant, told what had happened.

Not four hours after the hands had ridden in to the Circle Squared the entire ranch-house and its outbuildings had been surrounded by shadowy Apache riders who arrived with the dusk.

"It was right spooky," said the fungus-faced oldster, rubbing at his wrists and ankles and glancing around at his companions for confirmation of his view, "like they was dead. Not a sound out of any of 'em, and all kinda glowin' with that faint, silvery light."

"Natural phosphorescent paint found in the Guadalupe Mountains of New Mexico can give that effect. It is a favorite warpaint of the Kakatanawa Apache and is said to scare the bejeezus out of their enemies." The Masked Buckaroo helped Windy outside to his usual rocking chair.

"Well, boss, I guess it scared the shit out of us, too," said Windy philosophically, "because we was impressed. Especially when they didn't attack. They seemed to be darin' us to shoot at 'em. This stand-off went on for a couple of hours and then they kinda faded back into the darkness. We didn't feel too easy about this and were waiting for their next trick when this mist came up, all of a sudden, and we heard this single voice calling against a wild wind. My blood ran colder than a Wyomin' weasel..."

"He's right, boss," confirmed the usually-skeptical Pinto Pete. "It did things to yore insides, that singin'."

"Couldn't have been worse than Windy's yodeling." Shorty winked at his old friend.

"Come to think of it, it *did* sound a little bit familiar!" The Breed Papoose joined in the fun.

"Well," said Windy, "I don't know about the rest of you boys, but I was barely in control of my bowels *or* my bladder."

Suddenly sober, the experienced old hands nodded their agreement. The scene, the noise, the fog had all combined to terrify them and somehow blind them to the fact that the Indians were sneaking into the compound, weaving in with the mist, getting through the doors and taking over the entire ranch without a single blow falling or a shot fired. When the boys got a hold of themselves again, they found Miss Jenny and Don Lorenzo in the hands of the Apache and they were tied up, sitting on a table. There appeared to have been no time passed between the events. They did not feel they had slept or that they had been drugged.

"It was more like a dream," said Grumpy, after some thought. "Like magic might be..."

"Yet it didn't seem bad or crazy, did it?" said Pinto Pete. "We weren't threatened..."

"They took Jenny and Don Lorenzo," said the young vigilante very quietly, his steel-blue eyes glittering behind his mask. "I would call that an act of aggression, I think."

"But they didn't seem scared, either," offered Windy. "And I can always tell, boss, when Miss Jenny's scared."

This set the Masked Buckaroo to thinking for a moment. Then he was forced to put intellectual speculation behind him and turn to more pressing action. The Indians had been gone only three or four hours and had left a substantial trail, heading South West, towards the US border. The Buckaroo had no trouble following. Not for nothing was he respected by the Kakatanawa as "Pa-ne-e-ha-ha-ska-na-o-nee-pa-no" or *Sniffing Dog.*

"They have made no attempt to hide their trail. This in itself is significant," said the Buckaroo, reining in on a bluff as a vast, bloody sunset turned them all into black silhouettes and the yellow sky darkened against the blue of the night to reveal a silver wash of stars. He pushed back his sombrero and brushed dust from his face. "They mean for us to follow them."

As soon as his loyal riders were gathered around him the Masked Buckaroo explained his strategy. They would camp here for the night, but the two men with the freshest mounts would ride out before dawn racing for Port Sabatini via San Antonio with all the information Colonel R.G. 'Thunderclap' Meadley could be given. Once they had delivered their messages to Colonel Meadley in San Antonio they would then ride to see Captain Blackgallon Jones, the Welsh Engineer, and hand over the remaining documents.

"The army has some of the best modern inventions at its disposal," the Buckaroo assured his audience. "The wild Indian of today has little chance against such resources. Now we shall see Texas' investment in modern technical innovation paying off.

"But meanwhile," he reminded his listeners, his voice growing deeper and sterner and his fists hardening about Brenda's reins, "my wife and oldest friend are prisoners of these mysterious 'Ghost Warriors' and my guess is they're luring us into a trap."

"But why?" The Breed Papoose had already dismounted and was lifting the saddle off his tired bronc. "They could've taken us all at the ranch. They only had to wait for you, Buckaroo."

"That's what's puzzlin' me," admitted the young vigilante, "and that ain't the only thing. There's a whole lot to this affair that stinks higher than a Pecos fish pond in August. No Apache I ever came across behaved like these hombres. Sarajevo, did you ever get to see any of the atrocities you heard they'd committed?"

Sarajevo removed his battered sombrero and scratched his head. "I can't say I did, boss."

"And did you meet anyone who had seen anything at first hand?"

Sarajevo frowned and thought back carefully. After a while he shook his head. "Nope."

"What are you drivin' at, boss?" the Papoose wanted to know.

But the Buckaroo was not yet ready to speak. While the others made camp, he took his portable writing kit from his saddle-bags and penned messages to the necessary personnel. This done, he sealed each envelope, then stretched out with his head on his saddle to sleep.

The Buckaroo was up before his companions, waking them to the smell of fresh coffee on a boisterous fire. Soon Windy had un-limbered his pans and provisions and was preparing the hearty break-fast all the boys looked forward to when on the trail. Then messengers were dispatched, full of ham, eggs, beans and java, riding like the wind, and the Buckaroo issued instructions to his remaining men.

Soon the little party on the bluff was reduced by a further two. As the sun rose into a blue, misty sky and moonhawks sailed far overhead, the Masked Buckaroo, and his loyal companion Windy O'Day, continued on the trail the Apache had left for them. Tex knew he was taking a chance, but he was a natural born gambler. He was staking not only his own life and that of his companion, he was staking the liberty and well-being of his wife and mentor.

Soon the two partners were the only moving objects to be seen for scores of miles in that bleak landscape on which the sun fell with savage intensity, casting the long shadows of cactus and jebediah-tree across the stirring dirt. Yet the Apache trail was impossible to lose.

"They've driven a highway for us," said Windy, still puzzled. He was used to having a harder time than this tracking Apache. "Is this a band sent to draw us off while something bigger happens somewhere else?"

"I've allowed for the possibility, Windy," the Buckaroo reassured the old-timer. "Modern communications coupled with the most up-to-date transport systems should solve that particular problem, also. But the mystery remains — why and where are they leading us and for what purpose."

"Maybe just one of their devilish tricks," suggested Windy. "Who can figure what goes on in the head of an Apache?"

"I guess I can usually take a pretty good guess," Tex drawled modestly. He had, after all, lived the life of an Apache brave and gone through the harshest trials of manhood to the approval of his blood-brothers. In other words, Tex *could* think like an Indian. This affair, however, baffled him.

An hour later they arrived at the Telegraph Station to find it a gutted, smouldering shell. The wires had been cut and used to bind the operator and his wife. The couple had been laid across the nearby tram-tracks which had been dynamited and were unuseable from this point on. Their personal property had been removed from the station and piled nearby on the line as if the thief had ridden off in haste.

As the Buckaroo swung out of his saddle and stopped to cut the man and woman free he looked meaningfully at Windy. "Ever hear of the Apache doing this?" he asked.

Windy scratched at his tangled beard and frowned hugely. "Can't say I ever did, boss."

The telegraph operator was, as so many in his profession, a mute, but his pretty and agreeable young wife spoke enough for both of them. Not that she had any clear idea what had happened to her. The Indians had turned up out of nowhere and surrounded the station. "They just sat there on their ponies, staring in at us." They had the look of ghosts, she said, but she guessed they were wearing some kind of warpaint. Their leader carried a massive black-bladed warlance and had, she would swear, the eyes of the devil — "Red and glaring like the fires of hell!" She apologized for her language.

"Ma'am," said the Buckaroo quietly. "There are some experiences which call for strong expression. I suspect this is one of them. What happened next?"

She was not sure. She spoke of a silvery mist growing so thick that it crept into the cabin and filled the room. It had a faint smell, like vanilla. In some way she could not quite remember the Apache had entered the station. The chief had spoken a few words, but she had not understood them. The sound was awful. It made something inside her head hurt.

She had been lying on the tracks, watching the fire, before she wondered what had happened to them. Although she was unable to remember the events, it did not seem to her that they had ever actually occurred. It was, she said, as if certain things had simply not happened.

"As if Time itself had been cut up at random and then put back together again with pieces missing?" suggested the Masked Buckaroo.

"Exactly," she gasped. "How did you know?"

But the young Texan did not reply. His mind was elsewhere. He was trying to recall a book he had read long ago while at school in England. The book had been in old German and had been given to him to study. But he had become fascinated by its arguments and its odd narrative. There was something about this business which reminded him of that book, but he could not think what.

Remembering his manners, the Buckaroo touched his gloved hand to his hat. "Just a hunch, really," he answered. "Well, ma'am, we're expecting a track-mendin' team along soon. I don't expect you'll be bothered by the Apache again. Are you willin' to wait here until the army arrives?"

"Since your trail clearly leads after the Indians," she said, "I think I would prefer to await the army." She went to help her balding, red-faced little husband to his feet. She dusted at him vaguely with a cloth. Beaming, he accepted this attention as a show of affection.

"Excellent!" exclaimed the young Texan, taking out his writing set. "I will leave a message with you. It can be dispatched as soon as Colonel Meadley's 'Flyin' Tracklayers' arrive and fix everything up."

Clearly delighted that the famously romantic old soldier was on his way, the woman accepted the envelope the Buckaroo handed her.

A moment later Tex was mounted again. Brenda's forelegs flailed the air. She was impatient to be off.

"Good luck, Buckaroo!" The woman waved with the envelope as Tex and Windy disappeared rapidly in a dust-cloud of their own making.

Chapter Three
The English Detective

HOURS LATER, after following a waddy for a few miles, they found themselves in semi-desert, with nothing but the jaspers, mesquite and tumbleweed for company. In the far distance was a scattering of bluffs while even further away they made out the faint, blue outline of a mountain range. They reined in to take stock of the trail. It looked as if the Indians were heading for the mountains. There was still daylight left and they determined to press on while they could.

Windy O'Day was uncertain, however. "What if these redskins are leading us off so they can do something really bad?" he proposed.

"I have sent the appropriate messages, Windy." The Buckaroo brandished a grey glove he had discovered on the trail. "This means they're leading us to Jenny," he said. "And, old pard, that's all I reckon I care about just now..."

It was not a sentiment Windy could disagree with.

He was about to reply when a voice sounded behind them, startling them both.

Tex whirled in his saddle, his fingers falling to the handles of his revolvers. Then he relaxed, laughing.

"There's only one hombre could sneak up on The Masked Buckaroo like that," he said with admiring respect as he stuck out his hand and addressed the newcomer. "And that's Sir Sexton Begg! Good evening, my old friend. What brings you to this part of the prairie?"

It was indeed the famous English detective, who had last worked with The Masked Buckaroo on the exhilarating *Case of the Glass Armadillo* when the two lawmen had joined forces to solve a particularly sticky mystery and overturned some pretty ornery hombres in the process.

Sir Sexton was dressed for the bush, with a wide-brimmed hat, hunting whites and a voluminous dust-coat. His horse was a sturdy black Arab. In her long holsters were two rifles — a Winchester and a Purdy's — and the rest of the detective's simple kit was rolled behind the saddle. He himself was an aquiline man in middle-years, lean and fit and with an alertness of bearing which might have belonged to a much younger individual. His chiseled features emphasized the eagle-sharpness of his grey-blue eyes, displaying a superb intelligence — one that for many years had been used to singular effect against the criminal fraternity.

"I picked you up a couple of hours ago," the detective told his friend. "And because I couldn't initially be sure it was you, I took my time before revealing myself. Besides, I rather enjoyed the fun of wondering when you'd spot me."

"I couldn't want a better companion in this escapade," declared the young Buckaroo. "But what are you doing here, Sir Sexton, if I might ask?"

"I would guess it is what you are doing," the detective replied. "I am on the trail of a first-class trouble-maker."

"Would he be known by any chance in these parts as Pale Wolf?" asked the Buckaroo.

"That is not the name by which he is most familiar to me," declared the detective, "but I am aware of it. What is your business with him?"

Laconically, the Masked Buckaroo recounted the events of the last couple of days.

As they continued to ride, Sir Sexton took out his big onyx pipe and packed it full of his favorite M&E. Soon the surrounding air was filled with the wonderful smell of aromatic ope.

"It certainly doesn't sound like Apaches," interrupted Windy, after the Buckaroo had finished his tale.

"Well, I think you'll find Apaches are involved." Sir Sexton gestured with the pipe. "And perhaps more than you have bargained for. You are right, however, in suggesting that these are not Apache tactics. They are, in fact, the tactics of the man I seek."

"And who is that?" Tex squinted his eyes against the darkling sky. It was no longer possible to see the range, but the buttes stood black and tall with the sun behind them.

"I am not sure he has a name you would recognise, Tex," said Sir Sexton. "Save one, of course. His Kakatanawa Apache name."

"Lib-nu-pa-na-da?"

"He is called that in many languages. I mean the name he has adopted."

"Ulrucha?"

"Just so. For it is not his true name. He adopted it from the first Ulrucha — the man your father fought so long ago. That man was killed in a famous duel."

"I know the story," said the Buckaroo, "and I've seen the evidence for it. Ulrucha's long, white scalp hung in my father's smoking shed for a number of years. Until I gave it back to the Apache."

"You gave it back? Aha!"

It was growing too dark to ride and the three men headed for a sheltered gulch, making camp some distance from the water and preparing the surrounding ground against the mob of varmints which would be attracted to them in the night. Windy O'Day had soon cooked up a tasty meal and they ate in silence for a while, looking up at the bright stars and listening to the distant song of the coyotes.

"There's nothing like a night spent under the stars in the American wilderness," said Sir Sexton, offering his pouch of M&E to his friends.

They agreed enthusiastically as they packed their pipes.

Soon all three men were smoking thoughtfully, their eyes on imagined scenes, as they considered their situation.

After some time, Windy spoke. "I reckon they ain't hostiles at all," he said. "Not in the regular sense, anyway."

"Your instincts are perfect as always, Windy," said Sir Sexton. "How do you explain their apparent ability to make themselves invisible?"

"If Indians believe they're invisible, sometimes that's enough. They're so tricky at not being seen, anyway..."

But even Windy realized his explanation did not fit the stories they had heard — let alone his own experience. "I just can't see how they slipped past us. Hardly a man in the bunkhouse ain't an experienced Injun fighter — and Don Lorenzo knows more about Apache than Geronimo. Yet we wasn't drugged. Unless there was somethin' in that smoke."

"It's an old trick," Sir Sexton spoke almost abstractedly, his mind elsewhere. "Almost a favorite, I'd say."

"You mean you know how it was done, Sir Sexton?" Tex wanted to know.

"I believe I do, Tex. Indeed it is a timeless method. That isn't the mystery. What interests me is how he was able to employ it here."

"Were we drugged, Sir Sexton?" asked Windy, his whiskers bristling.

27

"Not exactly, Windy. I would guess we are dealing with forces which don't need to slip anyone a mickey finn in order to do their work. You may think me mad or worse, gentlemen, but I believe we are dealing with nothing less than the supernatural!"

"You mean we really are fightin' ghosts!" Windy's eyebrows leapt to join his unruly mop of grey hair.

"After a fashion." Sir Sexton fell again into a thoughtful silence, unable or unwilling to answer Windy's many questions.

Tex, too, said nothing, but stared into the heart of the fire. It was clear to Windy that his mind was not on supernatural speculation but on the fate of his beautiful young wife, Jenny. It was not the Buckaroo's way to make much of his personal fears, but there was no doubt he was in an agony of anxiety.

A little later, when the moon came out and turned the whole prairie into a silver fantasy, Sir Sexton got up. They saw him sit down on a rock to inflate an Association soccer ball. When they finally put their heads to their saddles, Sir Sexton was still out there amongst the cactus and the jerrymanda punting the ball expertly through the asymmetric goal-posts formed by an ancient yucca, muttering to himself, making complicated, almost mystical passes with the ball and puffing periodically on his vast pipe.

THEY WERE UP again before dawn and on the trail, with Tex leading the way. He was even more anxious than before to catch up with the men who had captured his wife. For the first time since he had set out in pursuit he was beginning to wonder if he would ever see her again.

Sir Sexton apologized if he had disturbed them with his activities. "I have a rule about exercise," he said. "Especially when I need to think something over. And, of course, usually I have a rod with me. But here —" With a helpless gesture he indicated the dusty, waterless plain over which they rode.

The mountains were now clearly distinguishable. The ancient, eroded peaks glowed like copper in the sunlight. They were the most south-easterly tip of the Nova Guadalupes, close to where they joined the Guadalupes proper.

As they rode, Sir Sexton explained what had brought him to this bleak plain.

Called upon to investigate the third theft of the Fellini Chalice, otherwise known as the Garth Cup, this time from the rooms of his own brother-in-law, the detective had uncovered an extraordinary story which had already brought him face to face with the Gateshead Leopard Men and the lost tin-miners of Cornwall, had him crawling through an endless succession of tunnels, storm-water drains, deep galleries, shafts and corridors in pursuit of his quarry.

"For most of my recent experiences, I must say, have taken place underground! A week ago you would have found me sailing the five great subterranean canals which meet at the Quai D'Hiver in Paris. It was rather a relief to take the express zeppelin to Austin and then ride alone under these wide skies."

"What led you to Texas?" asked the Masked Buckaroo, leaning to rebuckle a strap.

"That's a very long story indeed," Sir Sexton told him. "Suffice to say I am on the trail of the one who has been called Pale Wolf by the Apache. I believe he has gained possession of the Garth Cup and means to use it in a ceremony intended to increase, you might put it, the power of Chaos in our world!"

"Are we talkin' Loo-cif-her, here," Windy wanted to know.

"If you like," said the English detective.

29

The old-timer shuddered. "I can take pretty near anything the Apache want to try," he said, "but when it comes to devils an' ghosts, sir, I am not your man. I guess my brain don't believe in such things. But my feet never seem to listen to my brain."

Sir Sexton clapped a friendly hand upon the old man's shoulder. "Don't worry, Windy. You shan't be called upon to deal with such things. That's my business, I'm afraid."

"I ain't sure I'm much better at handling that stuff than Windy," said the Buckaroo doubtfully. "I must admit in my wildest dreams I didn't really believe old Ulrucha was a ghost!"

"He is not a ghost," Sir Sexton declared quietly. "I assure you, Tex, he is something far more powerful than that."

With a grim, distant expression, he urged his horse into a gallop and for a while raced ahead of his companions, lost in the contemplation of his own terrifying knowledge.

Chapter Four
The Will of the Wolf

THE THREE ADVENTURERS dismounted at the mouth of a towering canyon and looked in awe at the strange red limestone formations all around them. The Apache trail led relentlessly to this spot — and into the canyon. What Tex and his friends had to work out now was the kind of trap it was...

Although Tex's every instinct was to ride like fury into the canyon and with both guns blazing rescue his wife, he knew that he must continue to use his brains and self-control if he was going to get Jenny free.

High overhead, suddenly came the thin whine of an aero-engine.

Glancing upward they saw the dark blue and gold hull of a Texan flying battle-cruiser easing herself over a mountain peak and hovering above them.

This was all Tex needed to see. While Sir Sexton took out his pocket holograph and exchanged messages with the ship, he removed his Winchester from its scabbard and checked the rifle's action.

"Are we ready, Tex?" Windy wanted to know. He squared his shoulders, ready to face the Devil himself, if necessary, but not looking forward to the prospect.

"We sure are, Windy," declared the young cowboy. "But you ain't comin' with us, pard. I need you here to signal."

After a quick word of explanation, the Masked Buckaroo shook hands with the old-timer, grinned his famous go-to-hell grin, loosened his twin guns in their holsters and galloped to ride side by side with Sir Sexton Begg into the shadows of that vast canyon.

The silence was profound. All the men heard was the creak of their own harness, the sound of hoofs thudding with relentless rhythm into the soft sand of the canyon bottom. Very evidently, many horses had already come this way.

"I would guess there's maybe fifty warriors," Tex suggested, at Sir Sexton's question. "And then there's captives, maybe loot. The wagons ain't too heavily loaded and the horses pulling them are fresh enough. If I was readin' these signs as I usually would, I'd say it was a whole tribe, or at least a big village, on the move. Has he got his women and children with him, do you think?"

"Not his," said Sir Sexton.

Tex shuddered.

THE CANYON GREW steeper, taller and darker, and still the two men rode steadily on until at last they came to a place where the high limestone walls widened into a massive, rough circle.

From above, a great beam of sunlight poured down to give the effect of a spot, focused on the center of the clearing.

The shadows were full of restless shapes. Tex could smell them all around him, but he did not reveal this. He looked steadily ahead, trying to shield his eyes against the glare from the pool of light into which three silhouetted figures now moved, as if they had been waiting for him.

He immediately recognized the first figure as his beloved wife, Jenny. She was clearly unhurt and not especially frightened.

The second figure was Tex's wise old friend Don Lorenzo, his sombrero turned down against the blazing sunshine.

The third figure was a thin, muscular figure in an Apache breechclout and bolero jacket, a massive warlance in one hand, a repeating rifle in the other. He was far taller than the average Indian. His skin had a strange, silvery tinge so that Tex's first thought was 'the man's a leper!'

From the long, tapering, handsome skull stared two dark, crimson eyes which seemed to burn with fire so ancient it had petrified.

The war-lance was bigger than any Comanche weapon, with a wide blade of black iron burned with patterns of writhing ruby-red hieroglyph in no language either man recognized, perhaps some ancient Semitic alphabet. The man stared at them with a haughty almost bored expression. It was as if his chief attention were elsewhere, as if those strange, unsmiling eyes stared into another world than this.

Tex was immediately struck by the profound air of melancholy exuding from the man. He had the manner of someone who had lived for ten thousand years or more and had seen nothing to confirm any faith he might ever have had in the world's improvement.

SIR SEXTON BEGG rested in his saddle, his arms folded over his pommel, his reins loose in his hands. "Good afternoon, your highness," he said sardonically.

The Apache leader turned his head to regard Begg and his eyes seemed to narrow in a smile. "So you have found me, Sir Sexton. I had not expected to meet again so soon!"

"Always a pleasure." Begg took his pipe and baccy from his coat and offered the pouch to Pale Wolf who shook his head, declining gracefully.

As the detective filled his bowl and lit the mixture, puffing luxuriously, Tex could contain himself no longer. "I need to know, sir," he said to the War Chief, "if my wife and friend are your prisoners."

"No longer," said the Apache chief. "They are free from this moment. They have served their turn."

"And what turn was that, sir?" demanded Jenny sharply, moving rapidly to her husband's side. "You were never clear on the issue. Even at supper the other evening."

The Buckaroo dismounted to embrace her. Thankfully he shook hands with Don Lorenzo.

Pale Wolf smiled wistfully at Jenny's remark. "I apologize," he said. "My problem is not that I lie, but that the truth is unacceptable to most people. Sometimes it is impossible to disguise or even modify."

He spoke a melodic, vibrant, faintly-accented English which made it immediately clear how he could lead so many young warriors by the power of his words alone.

Then the great black war-lance was in his hands and the red engravings seemed to come alive within the metal, reflecting his blazing, ruby eyes, giving his face the sheen of a silver mask.

"Let us finish this," he said. He lifted his head to survey the peaks above.

And then he smiled.

Chapter Five
Apache Dreams

A S THE STRANGE albino lifted the war-lance to strike, the Masked Buckaroo pushed Jenny behind him and lifted one gloved hand.

From somewhere high above came the familiar notes of a Texan Cavalry cornet calling a complicated 'Alert'. The sound seemed to go on forever and the young vigilante looked on in astonishment as the silver-faced warrior drew back his long head, the white hair cascading and curling about his naked shoulders, to howl in sudden, impossible unison with the bugle's call.

Next the black blade itself began to vibrate and moan and give vent to that hideous crooning sound others had remarked. Hearing it made it almost impossible to hold down the contents of one's stomach. Yet gradually the pitch changed until it, too, sang in unison with the other voices.

So much was coming together in such harmony that it was impossible to believe Pale Wolf had not planned everything for this moment.

From out of the shadows now came a small, crooked individual, carrying a great jeweled chalice which, once the light from above touched it, also began to vibrate and sing in harmony with the bugle, the sword and the man.

Somewhere above a voice was calling — perhaps a warning. However, those in the canyon did not hear. Their attention was on the scene taking place under that concentrated beam of sunlight where a bizarre silver-skinned warrior in the full war-gear of a Kakatanawa Apache raised his voice in unnatural, inhuman music, performing a ritual which none doubted to be of the darkest, most powerful magic.

Then, as the echo of the bugle began to fade, the albino brought the great black blade down into the rock at his feet. His voice rose in hideous crescendo. The chalice held by the dwarf swelled and shattered and its glaring, silver light sliced down just as the black blade bit hard into the ground. A great fissure began to appear, forming a wide split and revealing the entrance of a cave from which a kind of boiling darkness erupted and then was gone.

Now from the opening came a series of stirrings, slitherings and whispers, all suddenly drowned by a deep, suffering groan, as if Mother Earth herself stirred in her sleep, dreaming of all the evil her children had done. And none there dared imagine what kind of creature bore such pain or uttered such sounds.

IT WAS SIR Sexton Begg who took the initiative. He stepped to the opening and stared down into it, frowning.

"So this is what you wanted," he said.

Behind him Pale Wolf smiled. "You have lost none of your courage, old enemy."

"Should I be afraid?" Sir Sexton looked up and met the Apache leader's strange eyes directly.

Pale Wolf shrugged. "I suppose not."

"I must congratulate you, sir," said Begg. "Your strategy is excellent. In the best traditions of the great Apache generals you have outmanoeuvered us. You guessed how young Tex here would act and think. You put yourself in his shoes, how he would cover all possible eventualities, leaving as little as possible to chance — because his wife's very soul could be at stake. You knew he would find a way to get the army here and that's exactly what he did..."

Pale Wolf reached into his breech-clout and removed a compact silver case. From this he took a small, brown cigaret and placed it between his lips. He lit it with a match and drew deeply of the dark smoke. He appeared to have nothing to do in the world but listen in a relaxed, easy posture, as Sir Sexton continued:

"You didn't want Jenny Brady. You didn't want Don Lorenzo. You didn't even want Tex himself. You wanted Tex's brains. You were using him to make sure the army would be here at a certain moment. And you didn't really want the army. You wanted the army trumpeteer. You did not really want the trumpeteer. You wanted his wonderful cornet which, of all the armies in the world, only the Texas Cavalry boasts. You did not actually want the cornet. You wanted a particular sequence of notes on that cornet which occurs in the formal 'Alert!' blown by Texas' bravest. And it had to sound at a particular moment, when the light fell in a certain way and when man, chalice and blade could give voice together, casting the great spell which would open the doorway you needed to the Realm Below."

At this the albino's eyes narrowed. His handsome features contained a strange, bitter amusement. His long-fingered hands, the color of bone, played with the ornate red shaft of the lance. "I believe I have underestimated you, however, Sexton Begg. For I did not anticipate your presence here. Neither did I prepare for it. Neither was I aware of your knowledge."

"Acquired in the course of a long investigation," murmured the detective. "I have been seeking you and the chalice for some while. Since you stole it from my brother-in-law, who had it on loan from the Sir John Soanes' Museum, three years ago. My brother-in-law was Curator of that Museum. He took his responsibilities seriously. The theft ruined him."

The albino seemed surprised and made as if to deny the charge, then shrugged and pulled deeply on his aromatic cigaret.

"Well, Sir Sexton, you could easily have thwarted me, it seems. Yet you did not. Why so?"

Begg pursed his lips and frowned, as if he had not considered the question before. At length he said: "Curiosity, I suppose. Which is after all my abiding and defining vice."

"Then I am obliged to you," said the albino, swinging the suddenly dormant blade onto his back and signaling to the people in the shadows.

Now as they emerged Tex saw that they were emaciated creatures, pale from every deprivation. They had the wretched, living-dead look of Reservation Indians. Their undernourished bodies spoke of terrible hardship. Their stance was the result of years of betrayal and institutional cruelty. But whereas the typical native had flat, hopeless eyes which stared neither into past nor future, these eyes were still alive. They misted with the first intimations of genuine salvation, all that this strange white-haired warrior had promised them when he told them to follow him, to obey him utterly, and he would lead them to the Realm Below, where herds of blond buffalo roamed prairies of waving, silver grass. They had obeyed him. He had used their shadowy forms to give the impression that whole war-parties roamed the South West. His tactics had been almost wholly psychological. Only in his mist-conjuring had he used magic.

With a faint smile on his handsome, alien lips, the albino continued to smoke as the tribe rode past. Already they were bearing themselves with a new self-respect. Men, women and children, wagons and horses, moved slowly down into the darkness. Invisible from above, they could be heard exclaiming with wonder and fresh confidence. What wonders were they seeing? What promise?

Those above ground were almost envious of those venturing below.

Jenny was the first to speak. "Are you saying, Pale Wolf, that you created this elaborate plan just to save these poor creatures?"

"I am not so altruistic, Mrs. Brady." The albino's red, glinting eyes were heavy with irony. "But I guessed my self-interest would combine with theirs to our mutual benefit. And so it proved."

"Have you deceived them in some hideous way?" murmured Don Lorenzo, his voice full of concern. "Where have you sent them?"

"Home," said the albino, tossing the remains of his cigaret into the shadows. "Home to the land of lost nations, of recollected pride and restored purpose. Home to the Reforgotten. Home to the Realm Below." His eyes met those of his old adversary. "Would you deny them that peace of mind, Sexton Begg? That pride?"

The English detective took an interest in his pipe. "My question has always been, your highness, whether you would deny me my peace of mind in achieving yours. It is the great fundamental debate. How do we achieve satisfactory compromise?"

"They intend you no harm," insisted the albino. "And as for myself, I believe you know how deeply uninterested I am in your race and its ambitions. As long as I am left alone."

"Left alone to murder and steal, sir," Sir Sexton Begg reminded the strange creature. "Why, you have killed half the British parliament! Lady Rhatchet herself dropped dead merely at the sight of you!

While this made you something of a popular hero, you are still guilty. You have stolen one of our great treasures and apparently destroyed it. You have put everyone, moreover, to a considerable outlay of time, concern and money which could have been better spent elsewhere. Sir, the rogue wolf is left alone only when he hunts in his own territory. I cannot believe you to be unaware of the fallacious nature of your arguments. You have not left us alone, sir."

At which a deep sigh escaped the albino's lips and he glared around impatiently. "Am I to be forever plagued by dullards and fools splitting hairs in abstract arguments? I am tired of the abstract, gentlemen. How I yearn for concrete!"

"I can offer you as much concrete, sir, as you please," said Sir Sexton Begg. "Her Majesty's prisons consist of little else."

The albino turned brooding eyes upward, studying the tiny figures who now rimmed the canyon. He spoke dreamily. "Did you bring the entire Texas army here, Mr. Brady? I am flattered. Please give Captain Gideon my compliments and tell him I shall have to meet him another time."

With that he mounted his pony and, without looking back, urged it at a rapid trot down into the fissure.

A few moments later they heard his vibrant, melodic voice from the echoing depths. The caverns enlarged and expanded it, giving it a rich, eternal bitterness, so that it seemed Satan himself addressed them in a voice full of tormented melancholy and longing.

"Farewell, old friend! We shall meet soon enough, no doubt, in the Realm Below!"

And then he was gone.

A MOMENT LATER a thin voice from the heights called down: "Could someone let us know what we're supposed to be doing?"

"All's well down here, Captain Gideon," Tex shouted back, and the echo reverberated through the depths and the heights 'giddy-on, giddy-on, giddy-on...' until it was spent.

Sir Sexton Begg continued to stare down into the fissure.

"Are you planning to follow them, Sir Sexton?" asked the young vigilante, half-joking.

"Not immediately," replied the detective, "though it is my duty. I know my limitations. I lack certain fundamental equipment supplied to field officers. I have no instinct for the underworld." He took a long pull on his pipe. "Yet that creature, that demon, as some believe him to be, can negotiate the most alien landscapes without any hesitation. Down there are inverted mountains which seem to hang by a thread from ceilings so distant they are lost in mist and gloom. There are canyons of slender spikes and crystallised forests and fields of cold colour. There are lakes of mercury and silver. Stone shapes writhe within viscous ponds and eyes, insane with the experience of aeons, stare out at you, asking impossible questions.

"Through all of this, our friend can sense routes and avenues which you and I could never find, even with maps and flares. The light down there is often dim. Sometimes it is not. There are whole series of caverns which glare with unbearable golden phosphorescence, creating a horrible heat. Some of these must be crossed to reach other lands of the Realm Below. He is not the only member of his family with such instincts. Some pass even more effortlessly between the worlds."

"But what is he?" asked Don Lorenzo, "If he is not the reincarnated Ulrucha the Indians believe him to be?"

"His family comes from Europe. They trace their lineage directly back to Anglo-Saxon times. Exiled by Ethelred (called the Unready) for daring to warn him of avertable danger, their ancestor was a Duke of Wessex. He was a strange man, accused of carnal knowledge of his own sister and damned by the Pope himself, and he traveled widely in the civilised lands of Arabia, learning all their sciences and lore. Eventually, I understand, he settled in Saxony, Germany, where he founded the present dynasty."

"So he has a family?" said Don Lorenzo, almost skeptically.

"A very large one. They are the von Beks."

"Wasn't there some scandal around them?" Jenny frowned.

"Many scandals, over the years. They have supplied the world with some interesting adventurers, male and female."

"But what *is* he?" Jenny wanted to know.

"His people are sometimes called 'eternals'," the detective replied slowly. "They are able to walk the roads between the worlds. The entire multiverse is theirs, yet some of them are still prisoners, still victims of their own stories. And some cannot die. For to die, an eternal must return to its own world, and that is not always possible. Some long for death. Some celebrate their longevity..."

"I am really not quite following this, Sir Sexton," said Jenny.

The detective gestured with his reins. "That is why, dear Mrs. Brady, I make so few attempts to offer explanations in a case of this kind. It is nothing to do, I assure you, with your intelligence. Your intelligence is extraordinarily high, as we know. But there are some things about our realities which only a certain number of people seem to be able to comprehend. And there is no persuading them. They simply cannot see what I see — or, indeed, that poor white-faced creature who has just left us can see."

"I do not believe I would want to see what he sees," said Don Lorenzo, lightening the atmosphere a little. "Especially at this moment."

"Oh, my dear sir," said Sexton Begg feelingly, "you do not know the beauty he experiences as he wanders the indescribable caverns of the Grey Fees where the organic and supernatural infrastructure of the planet inter-twine.

"He will see gorgeous jeweled halls so vast that twenty great cities stand in them, each upon a peak, high above the mercury rivers and bronze mists of the valleys which draw their light from phosphorescent rain dripping steadily from the distant roofs, making fresh formations, everywhere. Through these move the native folk of the Grey Fees, the *Offmoo,* so tall and thin and silent, in whispering robes and slender hoods, drifting like phantoms through their chattering rock forests and jingling crystal gardens, practising their rituals and legalities with obsessive, mindless insistence. And you have not heard the great natural organs playing. That is when all the cities make music at the same time and dying travelers come from thousands of miles to spend their last ecstatic hours borne upon so many wonderfully weaving melodies. There is no music more sophisticated nor more moving."

"Then should we not follow him this minute?" said Don Lorenzo a little drily. "Who could resist such a paradise?"

But Sexton Begg shook his head, refusing levity. "It remains, for all that," he said, "an *alien* paradise. It is an alternative.

"The Realm Below is a compendium of lost dreams. Defeated people arrived there, vowing return, revenge and all those other satisfactions with which we seem to perpetuate our miseries. But when they have been there for some time they become infected with a peculiar sadness. It is Pierrot's world, after all, without sunlight. That melancholy is characteristic of almost all the denizens of the Realm Below. Yet they live, they flourish, they have pride and their achievements are spectacular. All the great American civilisations are there, as well as the African, the Indian, even the Etruscan.

"For the Realm Below is where the defeated know triumph, where the disenfranchised and the marginalised find renewed power, where noble memory is made concrete and virtue is finally rewarded.

Where justice exists. Yet all but the *Offmoo* know that they are not native to the Realm, that they are forever exiled."

They were riding back up the canyon now. They could hear military voices raised in command, the busy clank and jangle of equipment.

"Do none of them ever yearn to return?" Jenny asked the detective.

"Some dream of it. Some even make plans for conquest of the Realm Above. But that pervasive melancholy usually informs their decisions. It is hard to make war while enjoying such emotions. They compensate for their lack of martial vigor by aspiring to a high standard of civilisation."

N OW THEY HAD reached the canyon's mouth again. But it seemed an age before they were out into open ground where Windy O'Day, his whiskers bristling with anxiety, sat expectantly, counting the riders as they emerged and brightening as soon as he saw their faces. Behind him now it was possible to see the practical magic Tex had worked, enabling Captain Gideon to get to the canyon hours ahead of the Apaches and position his men.

Nothing would have been possible, of course, without Colonel Meadley's famous 'Flying Tracklayers' who had laid a temporary bed across the prairie enabling Captain Blackgallon Jones to bring up his mighty double-decker war-trams loaded with men and ordnance.

These so called 'gun-tubs' with their electric gatlings could be of spectacular effect in plains conditions and had been employed to full effect at the Battle of El Paso against what Texas still insisted on called The Yankee Threat.

Express trams had transported the cavalry and now Captain Gideon's battle-hardened squadrons lined every vantage point of the surrounding country!

This vast display of military coordination brought a small smile to Sir Sexton's lips as he looked around him. He was too well-bred to observe what his companions also understood, that it had taken a great deal of organization and a great many men, not to mention a great deal of money, to ensure that a certain cornet note sounded at a certain moment in the wilds of the New Guadalupe mountains!

Two master-strategists had for a short time joined in a game whose rules were known only to one of them. Pale Wolf had used the Masked Buckaroo's famous strategic skills for his own purposes!

"I first smelled a rat," said Tex, "when I felt for that dog's pulse. The animal had died of natural causes, I am sure. The arrow had been shot into it much later. Did you notice that no-one was killed in those 'raids'? Nobody was even injured! And yet he used our old fears to make us work for him!" The Buckaroo could only admire the way in which he had been tricked.

He was not sure, however, the form his explanation would take when he came to talk to Captain Gideon and his men.

As if he had been struck by the same thought, Sir Sexton Begg leaned across in his saddle and murmured: "Remember what Pale Wolf said about not lying — that people usually could not understand the truth?"

The young vigilante nodded.

"Well," continued Sir Sexton, "I think we had best not explain all the details of how your dear ones were restored to you and what happened to Ulrucha and his miserable band. We had better speak of a 'secret pass' known only to the Indians.

Tex nodded in enthusiastic agreement. "No sense in stirrin' up speculation that won't go nowhere," he said. "But first you must tell me something more about that queer fellow 'Pale Wolf'. He's clearly not an Indian. He's definitely a white man. But he didn't look much like an average white, either. What is he, some kind of cross?"

"**H**E IS AT once the last and the first of his race," said Sexton Begg. "I should perhaps explain that he is a cousin of mine. We have ancestors in common. Though the family is named for Bek, it has always been associated with the principality of Waldenstein and its wonderful capital city, Mirenburg. There they intermarried with local aristocracy and share an intimate history with the place. For a while they ruled it. The man you met is Ulrich, Prince of Mirenburg, Count of Bek, who carries the ancient curse of the Bek blood..."

"Curse? More melodrama?" said Tex almost wearily. But the Englishman ignored him.

"Every few generations they gave birth to an albino. Every few centuries they gave birth to identical albino twins. And about every five hundred years they give birth to albino twins who are a girl and a boy. When that occurs there is a certain stir created in the occult world. A proliferation of magical swords is one phenomenon associated with such a birth."

"What are they?" asked Don Lorenzo in some distaste. "Vampires? Werewolves? What?"

"Some of them, as I said, are called 'eternals'. They live according to different rules and conditions but few have sinister ambitions where we are concerned. Indeed, they are often fairly altruistic. No others possess the warlock's powers you saw just now. But 'Monsieur Zenith', as that individual sometimes calls himself, is a master of magic, though his familiars are not always available to him here. His mind holds ancient secrets. His regular companions are the restlessly damned, the dispossessed, the abnormal. He consorts with criminals in the lowest dens of vice. And he plays Alkan and Liszt on the violin like an angel. No, Don Lorenzo, this is not an ordinary monster. Neither, in the usual sense, is he damned. I expect to meet him again. And when I do I hope I shall have the luck to best him.

Even extraordinary monsters, my dear sir, have no place in decent society."

"Which is why they deserve the freedom of the wild underworld at least," said the Masked Buckaroo with some feeling. He had been thinking over those events. "I think we should leave them alone. Why pursue them, Sir Sexton?"

The detective sighed. "Count von Bek — or Pale Wolf as you know him — is a criminal. It is my duty to bring him to justice. And that means I must follow him wherever he hides."

As if reminded of something, the Englishman rode over to have a word with Captain Gideon. The officer nodded rapidly and issued some instructions to his lieutenant. Soon several saddle-bags of supplies and equipment had been handed over to Sir Sexton who received them gratefully.

The detective brought his horse back, lifting his hat to Jenny. "Goodbye, Mrs. Brady. It has been a pleasure to meet you." He shook hands with the others who were rather concerned at this abrupt decision. They had not expected the detective to leave them so soon.

None asked him where he was going. They were not surprised, however, when he turned his horse about and began to ride into the shadows of the canyon on his way to the Realm Below.

They watched until he disappeared. "An hombre after my own heart, that Englishman," said the young vigilante. "I almost wish I was going with him."

"Where he goes, he goes alone, I think." Don Lorenzo removed his sombrero and wiped his forehead. He murmured some kind of prayer under his breath and crossed himself.

"Well, I seem to be the only one looking forward to getting home," said Jenny with a grin. "After this strange experience I'll never complain about the ordinary routines of the Circle Squared."

By now they had ridden up to where the tram-tracks began. Captain Gideon stepped forward, saluting.

The Masked Buckaroo thanked him for responding so rapidly and efficiently to his messages.

"You were right when you guessed the wires had only been cut nearby," said the captain. "Repairs were not difficult." The square-jawed army man lifted his hat to Jenny. "I'm glad we could be of help," he said warmly. "We look on you as a kind of a mascot in the Second and Third, ma'am." And, as he reined in his restless horse, there was a ghost of a blush on his neck and forehead.

"You will never appreciate the full extent of your help, captain," said the Buckaroo sincerely.

A S THEY CLIMBED the steps of the heavy war-tram and took their places on the mahogany seats, the young buckaroo put a strong and manly arm about his pretty wife's shoulders.

With an almost imperceptible jerk, the powerful electric motor was soon speeding them across the plains. Behind them a second tram collected track behind it, a demonstration of the skill and ingenuity of 'Thunderclap' Meadley's famous Flying Tracklayers and the daring imaginations of Blackgallon Jones's Welsh engineers. Together, they had done so much for Texas's military reputation.

Within hours they would be back at the Circle Squared.

Yet for all Jenny's talk of normality, the young avenger knew that life would never be quite the same again.

No matter how much he blocked it from his conscious mind, he would continue to dream of that subterranean world Sir Sexton called The Grey Fees.

Tex would long to experience those alien wonders. His curiosity would begin to grow within him until it filled him up like a fever.

He knew that one day that curiosity would get the better of him. He would give in to his impulse, pack his things into their battered old gunnies, saddle Brenda, and retrace the trail to the Realm Below.

Something in him hungered for that day, though he had no desire to leave Jenny behind. Something in him hungered for the echoing silences and silver prairies of the Grey Fees, where white buffalo grazed and ivory-colored horses galloped endlessly, where grey men hunted, their eccentric whistling circling around the granite clouds overhead and becoming a repeated, complex melody.

Something in Tex Brady would dream of it all until at last he made the dream reality.

He was not to know how soon that moment would come.

But that is another story.

THE END

NEXT MONTH:
Another great new
MASKED BUCKAROO adventure
from the lost files of
Warwick Colvin Jr.!
Don't Miss —
THE MASKED BUCKAROO in
THE DEVIL'S CAULDRON!

ABOUT MY MULTIVERSE

I THINK IT'S FAIR to say that I invented the Multiverse. John Clute in the *SF Encyclopedia* says John Cowper Powys (a Welsh writer for whom I have considerable admiration) used the term before me in *All and Everything,* but Powys, who could write me under the table, was really not using the term in the sense that I applied it — to describe a near-infinite nest of universes, each only marginally different from the next and only widely different when separated by millions of variants, where time is not linear but a field in which all these universes rest, creating the appearance of linearity within their own small sphere; where sometimes groups of universes exist in full knowledge and in full intercourse with the others, where 'rogue' universes can take sideways orbits, crashing through the dimensions and creating all kinds of disruptions in the delicate fabric of multiversal space-time.

Since the advent of Mandelbrot's extraordinary observations, the creation of Chaos Theory and Chaos Mathematics, I have been able to give further coherence to my notion, by suggesting we perceive each fresh 'plane' of the multiverse as a 'scale' - that scale alone differentiates them when so close together. The greater the variance of scales, the greater the variance of history and personal lives. Mass also changes with scale. We can also see the multiverse in terms of constantly renewing shoots and branches, growing more and more complex, each shoot a near-clone of the mother-branch, that branch in turn belonging to another and that to another until, a near-infinity of branches away, the trunk is joined. This fits best with observed reality but is much harder to visualise in linear terms.

I had already, from my earliest Elric stories, seen the world divided between Reason and Romance, Law and Chaos, and the Eternal Champion's inner struggles were reflected in his attempts to reconcile these elements, as most of us try to do in some form or another. All too often we are taught to believe we must abandon one impulse in order to give full attention to the other. Badly-educated people are suspicious of ambiguity and rational compromise. Something seems to have divided us. The old ideal of the Happy Mean, the perfect balance of interests and impulses, hardly ever seems to be aired, these days.

Come to think of it, nothing much of any substance at all is being aired these days. Everything seems in conflict and to no purpose. Modern radio and TV have rarely carried less real information to the public. The level of popular debate is at an all-time low. Instead, special interests engage in infantile propaganda wars, in graceless slanging matches, and call this free speech, offering the First Amendment as their noble authority. Modern newspapers care more for their threatened circulations than the truth. It seems to me that these days comics often play the part that SF once played when it had a vital and urgent purpose, of framing my generation's experience and helping it to understand what was actually going on, who was manipulating whom and why. That was and is popular art at its most vital. It's when romance engages with reality (as in the novels of Hammett and Chandler, say) that I'm attracted to a popular form, whether it be fiction or music or any other expression. It's the stuff that keeps its life long after its sell-by date. Its attack can be on the venality, cruelty and hypocrisy of authority, which gave the 17th and 18th century rogues' tales their enduring liveliness. It can be the furious anti-clericism, the outrage at the unseemly power of the Church, which fired so many of the 18th and 19th century 'Gothick' novels — those ancestors to all our modern supernatural adventure stories, whether they're about men with godlike powers or the fight against some hideous personification of undying evil, or both. It can be the consistent, coherent attacks on modern corporate cynicism and decadent political orthodoxy which mark so many of the best modern graphic novels. All reflect, respond and contribute to changes in the public's way of perceiving its world. That's how you can always tell the real thing. And that's what makes them so valued years after the brief flash of time in which they originally had to find a space in the market place.

For good or ill, Chaos Theory represents my experience and the Multiverse is an attempt to recreate it in all its variety. Although the Multiverse is a real place, it is also a metaphor and that for me is the real beauty — and usefulness — of it.

Welcome to my Multiverse — as familiar as it is strange.

THE FURTHER ADVENTURES
OF SHERLOCK HOLMES

I. The Adventure of the Texan's Honour
by John M. Watson, M.D.

I N CONSIGNING THESE papers to the care and consideration of History I am following the instructions of my friend, Sherlock Holmes, who desired that they be published, if published at all, one hundred years after the date of the last record, when those involved will be long dead and events so remote as no longer to embarrass living descendants. All the cases in question occurred during the years 1894 and 1895, when Holmes's reputation as a consulting detective was known to every street arab and peer of the realm, all of whom celebrated his recent 're-birth'. My reports in The Strand Magazine and later Collier's Magazine had captured the imagination of the civilised world. There was little doubt that my friend enjoyed his notoriety, though pretending to dismiss it. Fame brought him his choice of cases, enabling him to work for emperor or pauper, entirely dependent on the nature of the mystery, yet relieved him of all financial anxieties.

So many of Holmes's cases involved our absolute discretion that I have yet to set them down. Even those few I leave for posterity arouse feelings of acute discomfort when I think of their being published. No doubt I have nothing to fear and the Man of the Future, lounging in the comfort of his personal airship while his chauffeur drives him home from his office on the Moon, will have lost interest in such ancient scandals, especially if no hint of them ever reaches public ears.

Without further preamble, I consign these papers to the strong-box awaiting them, with instructions for my good friend, Sir Arthur Moorcock of Tower House, near Dent, to hold them in trust, and for his family to hold them in trust, until the year 1995, whereupon they may be published at the discretion of his descendants.

John M. Watson, M.D.

IT WAS ONE of those singularly hot Septembers, when the whole of London seemed to wilt from over-exposure to the sun, like some vast Arctic sea-beast foundering upon a tropical beach and doomed to die of unnatural exposure. Where Rome or even Paris might have shimmered and lazed, London merely gasped.

Our windows wide open to the noisy staleness of the air and our blinds drawn against the glaring light, we lay in a kind of torpor, Holmes stretched upon the sofa while I dozed in my easy chair and recalled my years in India, when such heat had been normal and our accommodation rather better equipped to cope with it. My house-keeper was visiting relatives in the Yorkshire Dales and I had been looking forward to some fly fishing. I had loaned my house to my brother-in-law and his family, who were in the process of moving. Meanwhile, a patient of mine was experiencing a difficult confine-ment and I had not in conscience been able to go far from London.

I had therefore been homeless and my friend, of course, had suggested I move back to Baker Street for the month until my own house became free again. I quickly settled in and enjoyed the opportunity to relive some of our adventures together. However, we had both planned to be elsewhere at this time and had confused the estimable Mrs. Hudson, who had expected Holmes himself to be gone.

Languidly, Holmes dropped the note he had been reading to the floor. There was a hint of irritation in his voice when he spoke.

"It seems, Watson, that we are, after all, to be evicted from our quarters. I had hoped this would not happen while you were staying."

My friend's fondness for the dramatic statement was familiar to me, so I hardly blinked when I asked: "Evicted, Holmes?" I understood that his rent was, as usual, paid in advance for the year.

"Temporarily only, Watson. You will recall that we had both intended to be absent from London at about this time, until circumstances dictated otherwise. On that initial understanding, Mrs. Hudson commissioned Messrs. Peach, Peach, Peach and Praisegod to refurbish and decorate 221b. This is our notice. They begin work next week and would be obliged if we would vacate the premises since minor structural work is involved. We are to be homeless for a fortnight, old friend. We must find new accommodations, Watson, but they must not be too far from here. You have your delicate patient and I have my work. I must have access to my files and my microscope."

I must admit I was not glad to hear the news. I had already suffered several setbacks to my plans and this fresh interruption, combined with the heat, shortened my temper a little. "Every criminal in London will be trying to take advantage of the situation," I said. "What if a Peach or Praisegod were in the pay of some new Moriarty?"

"Faithful Watson! That Reichenbach affair made a deep impression. It is the one deception for which I feel thorough remorse. Rest assured, dear friend. Moriarty is no more and there is never likely to be another criminal mind like his. I agree, however, that we should be able to keep an eye on things here. There are no hotels in the area fit for human habitation. And no friends or relatives nearby to put us up." It was almost touching to see that master of deduction fall into deep thought and begin to cogitate our domestic problem with the same attention he would give to one of his most difficult cases. It was this power of concentration, devoted to any matter in hand, which had first impressed me with his unique talents. At last he snapped his fingers, grinning like a Barbary ape, his deep-set eyes blazing with intelligence and self-mockery. "I have it, Watson. We shall, of course, ask Mrs. Hudson if she has a neighbour who rents rooms!"

"An excellent idea, Holmes!" I was amused by my friend's almost innocent pleasure in discovering, if not a solution to our dilemma, the best person to provide a solution for us!

Recovered from my poor temper, I rose to my feet and pulled the bell-rope.

Within moments our housekeeper, Mrs. Hudson, was at the door and standing before us.

"I must say I am very sorry for the misunderstanding, sir," she said to me. "But patients is patients, I suppose, and your Scottish trout will have to wait a bit until you have a chance to catch them. But as for you, Mr. Holmes, it seems to me that hassassination or no hassassination, you could still do with a nice seaside holiday. My sister in Hove would look after you as thoroughly as if you were here in London."

"I do not doubt it, Mrs. Hudson. However, the assassination of one's host is inclined to cast a pall over the notion of vacations and while Prince Ulrich was no more than an acquaintance and the circumstances of his death all too clear, I feel obliged to give the matter a certain amount of consideration. It is useful to me to have my various analytical instruments to hand. Which brings us to a problem I am incapable of solving — if not Hove, Mrs. Hudson, where? Watson and I need bed and board and it must be close by."

Clearly the good woman disapproved of Holmes's unhealthy habits but despaired of converting him to her cause.

She frowned to express her lack of satisfaction with his reply and then spoke a little reluctantly. "There's my sister-in-law's over at Number 2, Dorset Street, sir. I will admit that her cookery is a little too Frenchified for my taste, but it's a nice clean, comfortable house with a pretty garden at the back and she has already made the offer."

"And she is a discreet woman, is she, Mrs. Hudson, like yourself?"

"As a church, sir. My late husband used to say of his sister that she could hold a secret better than the Pope's confessor."

"Very well, Mrs. Hudson. It is settled! We shall decant for Dorset Street next Friday, enabling your workman to come in on Monday. I will arrange for certain papers and effects to be moved over and the rest shall be secure, I am sure, beneath a good covering. Well, Watson, what do you say? You shall have your vacation, but it will be a little closer to home than you planned and with rather poorer fishing!"

My friend was in such positive spirits that it was impossible for me to retain my mood and indeed events began to move so rapidly from that point on, that any minor inconvenience was soon forgotten.

Our removal to Number Two, Dorset Street, went as smoothly as could be expected and we were soon in residence. Holmes's untidiness, such a natural part of the man, soon gave the impression that our new chambers had been occupied by him for at least a century. Our private rooms had views of a garden which might have been transported from Sussex and our front parlour looked out onto the street, where, at the corner, it was possible to observe customers coming and going from the opulent pawn-brokers, often on their way to the Wheatsheaf Tavern, whose 'well-aired beds' we had rejected in favour of Mrs. Ackroyd's somewhat luxurious appointments. A further pleasing aspect of the house was the blooming wisteria vine, of some age, which crept up the front of the building and further added to the countrified aspect. I suspect some of our comforts were not standard. The good lady, of solid Lancashire stock, was clearly delighted at what she called 'the honour' of looking after us and we both agreed we had never known better attention. She had pleasant, broad features and a practical, no nonsense manner to her which suited us both. While I would never have said so to either woman, her cooking was rather a pleasant change from Mrs. Hudson's good, plain fare.

And so we settled in. Because my patient was experiencing a difficult progress towards motherhood, it was important that I could be easily reached, but I chose to spend the rest of my time as if I really were enjoying a vacation. Indeed, Holmes himself shared something of my determination, and we had several pleasant evenings together, visiting the theatres and music halls for which London is justly famed. While I had developed an interest in the modern problem plays of Ibsen and Pinero, Holmes still favoured the atmosphere of the Empire and the Hippodrome, while Gilbert and Sullivan at the Savoy was his idea of perfection. Many a night I have sat beside him, often in the box which he preferred, glancing at his rapt features and wondering how an intellect so high could take such pleasure in low comedy and Cockney character-songs.

The sunny atmosphere of Number 2, Dorset Street actually seemed to lift my friend's spirits and give him a slightly boyish air which made me remark one day that he must have discovered the 'waters of life', he was so rejuvenated. He looked at me a little oddly when I said this and told me to remind him to mention the discoveries he had made in Tibet, where he had spent much time after his struggle with Professor Moriarty. He agreed, however, that this change was doing him good. He was able to continue his researches when he felt like it, but did not feel obliged to remain at home. He even insisted that we visit the kinema together, but the heat of the building in which it was housed, coupled with the natural odours emanating from our fellow customers, drove us into the fresh air before the show was over. Holmes showed little real interest in the invention. He was inclined to recognise progress only where it touched directly upon his own profession. He told me that he believed the kinema had no relevance to criminology, unless it could be used in the reconstruction of an offence and thus help lead to the capture of a perpetrator.

We were returning in the early evening to our temporary lodgings, having watched the kinema show at Madame Tussaud's in Marylebone Road, when Holmes became suddenly alert, pointing his stick ahead of him and saying in that urgent murmur I knew so well, "What do you make of this fellow, Watson? The one with the brand new top hat, the red whiskers and a borrowed morning coat who recently arrived from the United States but has just returned from the north-western suburbs where he made an assignation he might now be regretting?"

I chuckled at this. "Come off it, Holmes!" I declared. "I can see a chap in a topper lugging a heavy bag, but how you could say he was from the United States and so on, I have no idea. I believe you're making it up, old man."

"Certainly not, my dear Watson! Surely you have noticed that the morning coat is actually beginning to part on the back seam and is therefore too small for the wearer. The most likely explanation is that he borrowed a coat for the purpose of making a particular visit. The hat is obviously purchased recently for the same reason, while the man's boots have the 'gaucho' heel characteristic of the south western United States, a style found only in that region and adapted, of course, from a Spanish riding boot. I have made a study of human heels, Watson, as well as of human souls!"

We kept an even distance behind the subject of our discussion. The traffic along Baker Street was at its heaviest, full of noisy carriages, snorting horses, yelling drivers and all of London's varied humanity pressing its way homeward, desperate to find some means of cooling its collective body. Our 'quarry' had periodically to stop and put down his bag, occasionally changing hands before continuing.

"But why do you say he arrived recently? And has been visiting north-west London?" I asked.

"Clearly our friend is wealthy enough to afford the best in hats and Gladstone bags, yet wears a morning coat too small for him. It suggests he came with little luggage, or perhaps his luggage was stolen, and he had no time to visit a tailor. Or he went to one of the ready-made places and took the nearest fit. Thus, the new bag, also, which he no doubt bought to carry the object he has just acquired. He did not realise how heavy it was. I am sure if he were not staying nearby, he would have hired a cab. He could be regretting his acquisition, especially if it were costly and not entirely what he was expecting. He certainly did not realise how awkward it would be to carry, especially in this weather. That suggests that he believed he could walk from Baker Street Underground Railway Station, which in turn suggests he has been visiting north west London, which is the area chiefly served from Baker Street."

It was rarely that I questioned my friend's judgements, but privately I found this one too fanciful. I was a little surprised, therefore, when I saw the top-hatted gentleman turn left into Dorset Street and disappear. Holmes immediately increased his pace. "Quickly, Watson! He must be close to his destination."

R ounding the corner, we were just in time to see the American arrive at the door of our own lodgings, Number 2, Dorset Street, and put a latch-key to the lock!

"Well, Watson," said Holmes in some triumph. "Shall we attempt to verify my analysis?" Whereupon he strode up to our fellow lodger, raised his hat and offered to help him with the bag.

The man reacted rather dramatically, panting like an animal, falling backwards against the railings and almost knocking his own hat over his eyes.

He glared at Holmes, and then with a wordless growl, pushed on into the front hall, lugging the heavy Gladstone behind him and slamming the door in my friend's face. Holmes lifted his eyebrows in an expression of baffled amusement. "No doubt the efforts with the bag have put the gentleman in poor temper, Watson!"

Once within, we were in time to see the man, hat still precariously on his head, heaving his bag up the stairs. The thing had come undone and I caught a glimpse of silver, the gleam of gold, the representation, I thought, of a tiny human hand. When he recognised us he stopped in some confusion, then murmured in a dramatic tone:

"Be warned, gentlemen. I possess a revolver and am an expert shot!"

Holmes accepted this news gravely and informed the man that while he understood an exchange of pistol fire to be something in the nature of an introductory courtesy in Texas, in England it was still considered impolitic to support one's cause by letting off guns in the house. This I found a little hypocritical from one given to target practice in the parlour!

However, our fellow lodger looked suitably embarrassed and began to recover himself. "Forgive me, gentlemen," he said. "I am a stranger here and I must admit I'm rather confused as to who my friends and enemies are. I have been warned to be careful. How did you get in?"

"With a key, as you did, my dear sir. Doctor Watson and myself are guests here for a few weeks."

"Doctor Watson!" The man's voice established him immediately as an American. The drawling brogue identified him as a South Westerner and I trusted Holmes' ear enough to believe that he must be Texan.

"I am he." I was mystified by his evident enthusiasm but illuminated when he turned his attention to my companion.

"Then you must be Mr. Sherlock Holmes! Oh, my good sir, forgive me my bad manners! I am a great admirer, gentlemen. I have followed all your cases. You are, in part, the reason I took rooms near Baker Street. Unfortunately, when I called at your house yesterday, I found it occupied by contractors who could not tell me where you were. Time being short, I was forced to act on my own account. And I fear I have not been too successful. I had no idea that you were lodging in this very building!"

"Our landlady," said Holmes dryly, "is renowned for her discretion. I doubt if her pet cat has heard our names in this house."

The American was about thirty-five years old, his skin turned dark by the sun, with a shock of red hair, a full red moustache and a heavy jaw. If it were not for his intelligent green eyes and delicate hands, I might have mistaken him for an Irish prize fighter.

"I'm James Macklesworth, sir, of Galveston, Texas. I'm in the import-export business over there. We ship all the way to Austin, our state capital, and have a good reputation for honest trading. My grandfather fought to establish our Republic and was the first to take a steam-boat up the Colorado to trade with Port Sabatini and the river-towns." In the manner of Americans, he offered us a resume of his background, life and times, even as we shook hands. It is a custom necessary in those wild and still largely unsettled regions of the United States.

Holmes was cordial, as if scenting a mystery to his taste, and invited the Texan to join us in an hour, when, over a whiskey and soda, we could discuss his business in comfort.

Mr. Macklesworth accepted with alacrity and promised that he would bring with him the contents of his bag and a full explanation of his recent behaviour.

Before James Macklesworth arrived, I asked Holmes if he had any impression of the man.

Holmes said that he found the Texan interesting and, he believed, honest. But he could not be sure, as yet, if he were acting out of character. "For my guess is there is definitely a crime involved here, Watson, and I would guess a pretty big one. You have no doubt heard of the Fellini Perseus."

"Who has not? It is said to be Fellini's finest work — cast of solid silver and chased with gold. It represents Perseus with the head of Medusa, which itself is made of sapphires, emeralds, rubies and pearls. Wasn't it stolen?"

"Your memory as always is excellent, Watson. For many years it was the prize in the collection of Sir Geoffrey Macklesworth, grandson of the famous Iron Master, once said to be the richest man in England. Sir Geoffrey, I gather, died one of the poorest. He was fond

63

of art but did not understand money. This made him prey to many kinds of social vampires! In his younger years he was involved with the aesthetic movement, a friend of Whistler's and Wilde's. In fact Wilde was a good friend to him, attempting to dissuade him from some of his more spectacular excesses!"

"Macklesworth!" I exclaimed.

"Exactly, Watson." Holmes paused to light his pipe, staring down into the street where the daily business of London continued its familiar round. "The thing was stolen about ten months ago. A daring robbery which left no clues. Inspector Lestrade believes it was spirited from the country and sold abroad. Yet I recognised it — or else a very fine copy — in that bag James Macklesworth was carrying up the stairs. He would have read of the affair, I'm sure, especially considering his name. Therefore he must have known the Fellini statue was stolen. Yet clearly he went somewhere today and returned here with it. Why? He's no thief, Watson, I'd stake my life on it."

"Let us hope he intends to illuminate us," I said as a knock came at our door.

M r. James Macklesworth was a changed man. Bathed and dressed in his own clothes, he appeared far more confident and at ease. His suit was of a kind favoured in his part of the world, with a distinctly Spanish cut, and he wore a flowing tie beneath the wings of a wide-collared soft shirt, a dark red waistcoat and pointed oxblood boots. He looked every inch the romantic frontiersman.

He began by apologising for his costume. He had not realised, he said, until he arrived in London yesterday, that his dress was unusual in England. We both assured him that his sartorial appearance was in no way offensive to us. Indeed, we found it attractive.

"But it marks me pretty well for who I am, is that not so, gentlemen?"

We agreed that in Oxford Street there would not be a great many people dressed in the fashion of the prairies.

"That's why I bought the English clothes," he said. "I wanted to fit in and not be noticed. The top hat was too big and the morning coat was too small. The trousers were the only thing the right size. The bag was the largest of its shape I could find."

"So, suitably attired, as you thought, you took the Metropolitan Railway this morning to — ?"

"To Willesden, Mr. Holmes. Good heavens! How did you know that? Have you been following me all day?"

"Certainly not, Mr Macklesworth. And in Willesden you took possession of the Fellini Perseus, did you not?"

"You know everything ahead of me telling it, Mr. Holmes! I need speak no more. Your reputation is thoroughly deserved, sir. If I were not a rational man, I would believe you were possessed of psychic powers!"

"Simple deductions, Mr. Macklesworth. One develops a skill, you know. But it might take a longer acquaintance for me to deduce how you came to cross some six thousand miles of land and sea to arrive in London, go straight to Willesden and come away with one of the finest pieces of Renaissance silver the world has ever seen. All in a day, too."

"I can assure you, Mr. Holmes, that such adventuring is not familiar to me. Until a few months ago I was the owner of a successful shipping and wholesaling business. My wife died several years back and I never remarried. My daughters are all grown now and married, living far from Texas. I was a little lonesome, I suppose, but reasonably content. That all changed, as you have guessed, when the Fellini Perseus came into my life."

"You received word of it in Texas, Mr. Macklesworth?"

"Well, sir, it's an odd thing. Embarrassing, too. But I guess I'm going to have to be square with you and come out with it. The gentleman from whom the Perseus was stolen was a cousin of mine. We'd corresponded a little. In the course of that correspondence he revealed the secret which now burdens me. I was his only living male relative, you see, and he had family business to do. There was another cousin, he thought in New Orleans, but he had yet to be found. Well, gentlemen, the long and the short of it was that I swore on my honour to carry out Sir Geoffrey's instructions in the event of something happening to him or to the Fellini Perseus. His instructions led me to take train for New York and from New York the *Arcadia* for London. I arrived yesterday afternoon."

"So you came all this way, Mr. Macklesworth, on a matter of honour?" I was somewhat impressed.

"You could say so, sir. We set high store by family loyalty in Texas. Sir Geoffrey's estate, as you know, went to pay his debts. My reason for seeking you out was connected with his death. I believe Sir Geoffrey was murdered, Mr. Holmes. Someone was frightening him and he spoke of 'financial commitments'. His letters increasingly showed his anxiety and were often rather rambling accounts of his fears that there should be nothing left for his heirs. I told him he had no direct heirs and he might as well reconcile himself to that. He did not seem to take in what I said. He begged me to help him. And he begged me to be discrete. I promised. One of the last letters I had from him told me that if I ever heard news of his death, I must immediately sail for England and upon arriving take a good sized bag to 18 Dahlia Gardens, Willesden Green, North West London, and supply proof of my identity, whereupon I would take responsibility for the 'Macklesworth birthright' and return immediately to Galveston."

"This I swore and only a couple of months later I read in the Galveston paper the news of the robbery. Soon after, there followed an account of poor Sir Geoffrey's suicide. There was nothing else I could do, Mr. Holmes, but follow his instructions, as I had sworn I would. However, I became convinced that Sir Geoffrey had scarcely been in his right mind at the end. I suspected he feared nothing less than murder. He spoke of people who would go to any lengths to possess the Fellini Silver, how I must keep our secret at all costs. He did not care that the rest of his estate was mortgaged to the hilt or that he would die, effectively, a pauper. The Silver was of overweening importance. I suspect the robbery and his murder are connected."

"But the verdict was suicide," I said. "A note was found. The coroner was satisfied."

"The note was covered in blood, was it not?" Holmes murmured as he lounged back in his chair, his finger tips together upon his chin.

"I gather so, Holmes, and since foul play was not suspected, no investigation was made."

"Quite so. Pray continue, Mr. Macklesworth."

"Well, gentlemen, I've little to add. All I have is a nagging suspicion that something is wrong. I do not wish to be party to a crime, nor to hold back information of use to the police, but I am honour-bound to fulfill my pledge to my cousin. I came to you not necessarily to ask you to solve a crime, but to put my mind at rest if no crime was committed."

"A crime has already been committed, if Sir Geoffrey announced a burglary that did not happen. But it is not much of one, I'd agree. What did you want of us in particular, Mr. Macklesworth?"

"Yesterday, I hoped that you or Dr. Watson might accompany me to the address — for obvious reasons. I am a law-abiding man, Mr. Holmes and wish to remain so. There again, considerations of honour —"

"Quite so," interrupted Holmes. "Now, Mr. Macklesworth, tell us what you found at 18 Dahlia Gardens, Willesden!"

"Well, it was a rather dingy row house, crowded with others of its kind along a little road about a quarter of a mile from the station. It was not what I had expected. Number 18 was dingier than the rest — a poor sort of a place altogether, with peeling paint, an overgrown yard, bulging garbage cans — the kind of thing you expect to see in the Houston slums, not in a suburb of London.

"All this notwithstanding, I found the dirty knocker and hammered upon the door until it was opened by an attractive woman of the octoroon persuasion. She was unusually tall, with broad shoulders and long, surprisingly well-manicured hands. Indeed, she was impeccable in her appearance, in distinct contrast to her surroundings. She was expecting me and introduced herself as Mrs. Gallibasta. I knew the name at once. Sir Geoffrey had often spoken of his housekeeper, in terms of considerable affection and trust. He had enjoined her, before he died, to perform this last loyal deed for him. She handed me a note he had written to that effect. Here it is, Mr. Holmes."

He reached across and gave it to my friend who studied it carefully. "You recognise the writing, of course ?"

The American was in no doubt. "It is in the flowing, slightly erratic, masculine hand I recognise. As you see I must accept the family heirloom from Mrs. Gallibasta and, in all secrecy, transport it straight back to America, where it must remain in my charge until such time as the other 'missing' Macklesworth cousin is found. If he has male heirs, it must be passed on to one of them at my discretion. If no male heir can be found, it should be passed on to one of my daughters — I have no living sons — on condition that they add the Macklesworth name to their own. I understand, Mr. Holmes, that to some extent I am betraying my trust. But I know so little of English society and customs. I have a strong sense of family and am proud to be related to such an illustrious line, but until Sir Geoffrey wrote and told me I had no idea we were so close. I feel obliged to carry out his last wishes. However, I cannot in conscience go without assuring myself that no foul play has been involved. I know that, of all the men in England, you will not betray my secret."

"I am flattered by your presumption, Mr. Macklesworth. Pray, could you tell me the date of the last letter you received from Sir Geoffrey?"

"It was undated, but I remember the post mark. It was the fifteenth day of June of this year."

"I see. And the date of Sir Geoffrey's death?"

"The thirteenth. I supposed him to have posted the letter before his death and that it was collected later."

"A reasonable assumption. And you are, of course, thoroughly familiar with Sir Geoffrey's hand-writing."

"We corresponded for several years, Mr. Holmes. The hand in this note is identical. No forger, no matter how clever, could manage those idiosyncrasies, those unpredictable lapses into barely readable words. But usually his hand was a fine, bold, idiosyncratic one. It was not a forgery, Mr. Holmes. And neither was the note he left with his housekeeper."

"But you never met Sir Geoffrey?"

"Sadly, no. He spoke sometimes of coming out to the ranch in Texas, but I believe other concerns took up his attention."

"Indeed, I knew him slightly some years ago, when we belonged to the same club. An artistic type, fond of Japanese prints and Scottish furniture. An affable, absent-minded fellow, rather retiring. Of a markedly gentle disposition. Too good for this world, as we used to say."

"When would that have been, Mr. Holmes?" Our visitor leaned forward, showing considerable curiosity.

"Some twenty years ago, when I was just starting in practice. I was able to provide some help in a case concerning a young friend of his who had got himself into trouble. I recall that Sir Geoffrey frequently showed genuine concern for the fate of his fellow creatures. He remained a confirmed bachelor, I understand. I was sorry to hear of the robbery. When the poor man killed himself, I was a little surprised that no foul play was suspected. A kindly sort of old-fashioned, unworldly man. The patron of many a destitute young artist. It was art — or at least artists — I gather, which so reduced his fortune."

"He did not speak much of art to me, Mr. Holmes. I fear he had changed considerably over the intervening years. The man I knew grew increasingly given to what seemed somewhat irrational anxieties. It was to quell these anxieties that I originally agreed to this scheme of his. I was honoured, Mr. Holmes, by the responsibility, but disturbed by what was asked of me."

"You are clearly a man of profound common sense, Mr. Macklesworth, as well as a man of honour. I sympathise entirely with your predicament. You were right to come to us and we shall do all we can to help!"

The relief of the American's face was considerable. "Thank you, Mr. Holmes. Thank you, Doctor Watson. I feel I can now act with some coherence."

"And Sir Geoffrey's housekeeper? What of her?"

"She intends to seek a new position in her native Spain. She will be glad to go home, she says. She came to Sir Geoffrey about five years ago, before he first wrote to me, and he always spoke of her in the most positive and grateful terms. A woman of some character who helped him marshal the last of his resources and kept him from the bankruptcy court. He spoke so warmly of her, sir, that I was bound to speculate on their relationship..."

"I take your meaning, Mr. Macklesworth. If what you suspect was the case, no doubt the class differences were insurmountable."

"I have no wish to impugn the name of my relative, Mr. Holmes."

"But we must look realistically at the problem, I think." Holmes gestured with his long hand. "I wonder if we might be permitted to see the statue you picked up today?"

"Certainly, sir. I fear the newspaper in which it was wrapped has come loose here and there —"

"Which is how I recognised the Fellini workmanship," said Holmes, his face becoming almost rapturous as the extraordinary figure was revealed. He reached to run his fingers over musculature which might have been living flesh in miniature, it was so perfect. The silver itself was vibrant with some inner energy and the gold chasing, the precious stones, all served to give the most wonderful impression of Perseus, a bloody sword in one hand, his shield on his arm, holding up the snake-crowned head which glared at us through sapphire eyes and threatened to turn us to stone!

"It is obvious why Sir Geoffrey, whose taste was so refined, would have wished this to remain in the family," I said. "Now I understand why he became so obsessed towards the end. Yet I would have thought he might have willed it to a museum — or made a bequest — rather than go to such elaborate lengths to preserve it. It's something which the public deserves to see."

"I agree with you completely, sir. That is why I intend to have a special display room built for it in Galveston. But until that time, I was warned by both Sir Geoffrey and by Mrs. Gallibasta, that news of its existence would bring immense problems — not so much from the police as from the other thieves who covet what is, perhaps, the world's finest single example of Florentine Renaissance silver. I intend to insure it for a million dollars, when I get home," volunteered the Texan.

"Perhaps you would entrust the sculpture with us for the night and until tomorrow evening?" Holmes asked our visitor.

"Well, sir, as you know I am supposed to take the *Arcadia* back to New York. She sails tomorrow evening from Tilbury. She's one of the few steamers of her class leaving from London. If I delay, I shall have to go back via Liverpool."

"But you are prepared to do so, if necessary?"

"I cannot leave without the Silver, Mr. Holmes. Therefore, while it remains in your possession, I shall have to stay." John Macklesworth offered us a brief smile and the suggestion of a wink. "Besides, I have to say that the mystery of my cousin's death is of rather more concern than the mystery of his bequest."

"I see we are of like mind. It will be a pleasure to put whatever talents I possess at your disposal, Mr. Macklesworth. Sir Geoffrey resided, as I recall, in Oxfordshire."

"About ten miles from Oxford itself, he said. Near a pleasant little market town called Witney. The house is known as Cogges Old Manor and it was once the centre of a good-sized estate, including a working farm. But the land was sold and now only the house and grounds remain. They, too, of course, are up for sale by my cousin's creditors. Mrs. Gallibasta said that she did not believe it would be long before someone bought the place. The nearest hamlet is High Cogges. The nearest railway station is at South Leigh, about a mile distant. I know the place as if it were my own, Mr. Holmes, Sir Geoffrey's descriptions were so vivid."

"Indeed! When, by the by, did you first contact him, sir?"

"It was Sir Geoffrey who first wrote me! He had an interest in heraldry and lineage. In attempting to trace the descendants of Sir

Robert Macklesworth, our mutual great-grandfather, he came across my name and wrote to me. Until that time I had no idea I was so closely related to the English aristocracy! For a while Sir Geoffrey spoke of my inheriting the title — but I am a convinced republican. We don't go much for titles and such in Texas — not unless they are earned!"

"You told him you were not interested in inheriting the title?"

"I had no wish to inherit anything, sir." John Macklesworth rose to leave. "I merely enjoyed the correspondence. I became concerned when his letters grew increasingly more anxious and rambling and he began to speak of suicide."

"Yet still you suspect murder?"

"I do, sir. Put it down to an instinct for the truth — or an over-wrought imagination. It is up to you!"

"I suspect it is the former, Mr. Macklesworth. I shall see you here again tomorrow evening. Until then, goodnight."

We shook hands.

"Goodnight, gentlemen. I shall sleep easy for the first time in months." And with that our Texan visitor departed.

"What do you make of it, Watson?" Holmes asked, as he reached for his long-stemmed clay pipe and filled it with tobacco from his familiar old slipper. "Do you think our Mr. Macklesworth is 'the real article' as his compatriots would say?"

"I was very favourably impressed, Holmes. But I do believe he has been duped into a venture which, if he obeyed his own honest instincts, he would never have considered. I cannot believe that Sir Geoffrey was everything he claimed to be or that you thought him to be. A frequenter of the more sensational bohemian gathering places! A patron of the arts. A philanthropist.

"Perhaps, but he was not a gentleman, if he sought to involve an innocent relative in a crime. Perhaps he was a better man when you

73

knew him, Holmes, but since then he has clearly degenerated. He keeps an octoroon mistress, gets heavily into debt and then plans to steal his own treasure in order to preserve it from creditors. He must have known how paramount family loyalties are in the Old South. Our Texan friend was bound to agree to Sir Geoffrey's request. I would not be surprised to discover that he is still abroad and conspired with his housekeeper to fake his own death."

"And gives his treasure up to his cousin? Why would he do that, Watson?"

"He's using Macklesworth to transport it to America. The Texan will not be suspected and will get the Silver easily to Galveston — where Sir Geoffrey can take back the thing at his leisure. It's monstrous, Holmes!"

"Well, Watson, it's not a bad theory and I suspect much of it is relevant."

"But you know something else?"

"I believe that Sir Geoffrey is dead. I read the coroner's report. He blew his brains out, Watson. That was why there was so much blood on the suicide note. If he planned a crime, he did not live to complete it."

"So the housekeeper, who was in his confidence, decided to continue with his plan?"

"There's only one flaw there, Watson. Sir Geoffrey appears to have anticipated his own suicide and left instructions with her. Mr. Macklesworth identified the handwriting. I read the note myself. Mr. Macklesworth has corresponded with Sir Geoffrey for years. He confirmed that the note was clearly Sir Geoffrey's."

"So the housekeeper is also innocent. We must look for a third party."

"We must take an expedition into the countryside, Watson." Holmes was already consulting his Bradshaw's. "There's a train from

Paddington in the morning which will involve a change at Oxford and will get us to South Leigh before lunch. Can your patient resist the lure of motherhood for another day or so, Watson?"

"Happily there's every indication that she is determined to enjoy an elephantine confinement."

"Good, then tomorrow we shall please Mrs. Hudson by sampling the fresh air and simple fare of the English countryside."

And with that my friend, who was in high spirits at the prospect of setting that fine mind to a decent problem, sat back in his chair, took a deep draft of his pipe, and closed his eyes.

We could not have picked a better day for our expedition. While still warm, the air had a balmy quality to it and even before we had reached Oxford we could smell the delicious richness of an early English autumn. Everywhere the corn had been harvested and the hedgerows were full of colour. Thatch and slate slid past our window which looked out to what was best in England whose people had built to the natural roll of the land and planted with an instinctive eye for beauty as well as practicality. This was what I had missed in Afghanistan and what Holmes had missed in Tibet, when he had learned so many things at the feet of the High Lama himself. Nothing ever compensated, in my opinion, for the wealth and variety of the typical English country landscape.

In no time we were at South Leigh station and able to hire a dog-cart with which to drive ourselves up the road to High Cogges. We made our way through winding lanes, between tall hedges, enjoying the sultry tranquility of a day whose silence was broken only by the sound of bird-song and the occasional lowing of a cow, the distant bark of a farm dog.

We drove through the hamlet, which was served by a Norman church, an Elizabethan public house and a Georgian grocer's shop which also acted as the local post office. High Cogges itself was reached by a rough lane, little more than a farm track leading past some picturesque thatched cottages, which were thickly covered with roses and honeysuckle, and seemed to have been there since the Day of Creation; a rather vulgar modern house whose owner had made a number of hideous additions in the popular taste of the day; a Jacobean farmhouse and outbuildings of the warm, local stone which seemed to have grown as naturally from the landscape as the spinney and orchard behind it. Then we had arrived at the locked gates of a thoroughly neglected Cogges Old Manor. It had been many years since the place was properly managed.

True to form, my friend began exploring and had soon discovered a gap in a wall through which we could squeeze in order to explore the grounds. These were little more than a good-sized lawn, some shrubberies and dilapidated greenhouses, an abandoned stable, various other sheds and a workshop which was in surprisingly neat order. This, Holmes told me, was where Sir Geoffrey had died. It had been thoroughly cleaned. According to reports Holmes had read on the train, Sir Geoffrey had placed his gun in a vice and shot himself through the mouth. At the inquest, his housekeeper, who had clearly been devoted to him, had spoken of his money worries, his fears that he had dishonoured the family name. The scrawled note had been soaked in blood and only partially legible, but it was clearly his.

"There was no hint of foul play, you see, Watson. Everyone knew that Sir Geoffrey led the Bohemian life until he settled here. He had squandered the family fortune on what Wilde referred to as *arsomania* and no doubt his many modern canvasses would become valuable, at least to someone, but at present the artists he had patronised had yet to realise any material value. I have the impression that half the denizens of the Café Royal depended on the Macklesworth millions until they dried up. I also believe that Sir Geoffrey was either distracted in his last years, or depressed. Possibly both. I think we must make an effort to interview the devoted Mrs. Gallibasta. First, however, let's visit the post office — the source of all wisdom in these little communities."

The post office/general store was a converted thatched cottage, with a white picket fence and a display of early September flowers which would not have been out of place in a Constable. Within the cool shade of the shop, full of every possible item from books to boiled sweets, we were greeted by the proprietress whose name over her doorway we had already noted.

Mrs. Piggott was a plump, pink woman in plain prints and a starched pinafore, with humorous eyes and a slight pursing of the mouth which suggested a conflict between her natural warmth and a slightly censorious temperament. Indeed, this is exactly what we discovered. She had known both Sir Geoffrey and Mrs. Gallibasta. She had been on good terms with a number of the servants, she said, although one by one they had left and had not been replaced.

"There was talk, gentlemen, that the poor baronet was next to destitute and couldn't afford new servants. But he was never behind with the wages and those who worked for him were loyal enough. Especially his housekeeper. She had an odd, distant sort of air, but there's no question she looked after him well and since his prospects were already known, she didn't seem to be hanging around waiting for his money."

"Yet you were not fond of the woman?" murmured Holmes, his eyes studying an advertisement for toffee.

"I will admit that I found her a little strange, sir. It wasn't her gypsy looks that bothered me, but we never sparked, if you follow me. She was always very polite and pleasant in her conversation. I saw her almost every day, too — though never in church. She'd come in here to pick up whatever small necessities they needed. She always paid cash and never asked for credit. It seemed that she was supporting Sir Geoffrey, not the other way around. Some said she had a temper to her and that once she had taken a rake to an under-footman, but I saw no evidence of it. She'd spend a few minutes chatting with me, sometimes purchase a newspaper, collect whatever mail there was and walk back up the lane to the manor. Rain or shine, sir, she'd be here. A big, healthy woman she was. She'd joke about what a handful it all was, him and the estate, but she didn't seem to mind. I only knew one odd thing about her. When she was poorly, no matter how sick she became, she always refused a doctor. She had a blind terror of the medical profession, sir. The very suggestion of calling Doctor Shapiro would send her into screaming insistence that she needed no 'sawbones'. Otherwise, she was what Sir Geoffrey needed, him being so gentle and strange and with his head in the clouds."

"But given to irrational fears and notions, I gather?"

"Not so far as I ever observed, sir. He hadn't changed since a boy. Though he stayed at the house for the past several years and I only saw him occasionally. But when I did he was his usual sunny self. You could tell from his expression that he thought the world of her, too. We thought she kept him young."

"That's most interesting, Mrs. Piggott. I am grateful to you. I think I will have a quarter-pound of your best bullseyes, if you please. Oh, I forgot to ask. Do you remember Sir Geoffrey receiving any letters from America?"

"Oh, yes, sir. Frequently. He looked forward to them, she said. I remember the envelope and the stamps. It was almost his only regular correspondent."

"And Sir Geoffrey sent his replies from here?"

"I wouldn't know that, sir. The mail's collected from a pillar-box near the station. You'll see it, if you're going back that way."

"Mrs. Gallibasta, I believe, has left the neighbourhood."

"Not two weeks since, sir. My son carried her boxes to the station for her. She took all her things. She's hoping to get a position in Las Cascadas, I gather. My boy mentioned how heavy her luggage was. He said if he hadn't attended Sir Geoffrey's service at St James's he'd have sworn he was in her trunk! If you'll pardon the levity, sir."

"I am greatly obliged to you, Mrs. Piggott." The detective lifted his hat and bowed. I recognised Holmes's brisk, excited mood. He was on a hot trail now, as he liked to say. "One last thing — would you recommend the beer at *The Mason's Arms?*"

"And the lunch, sir. It's all home-made."

The hostelry fulfilled our highest expectations of English country fare and while we enjoyed it Holmes refused to discuss the case. Only when we were leaving did he murmur: "I must go round to 221b immediately upon our return to London. I must consult some early files."

As I drove the dog-cart back to the station in the sweet-smelling afternoon air, Holmes scarcely spoke a further word. He was lost in thought all the way to London. I was used to my friend's moods and habits and was content to let that brilliant mind exercise itself while I gave myself up to the world's concerns in the *Telegraph*.

Mr. Macklesworth joined us for tea that afternoon. Mrs. Ackroyd had outdone herself with smoked salmon and cucumber sandwiches, small savouries, scones and cakes. The tea was my favourite Darjeeling, whose delicate flavour is best appreciated at that time in the afternoon, and even Holmes remarked that we might be guests at Sinclair's or the Grosvenor.

Our ritual was overseen by the splendid Fellini Silver which, perhaps to catch the best of the light, Holmes had placed in our sitting room window, looking out to the street. It was as if we ate our tea in the presence of an angel. Mr. Macklesworth balanced his plate on his knee wearing an expression of delight. "I have heard of this ceremony, gentlemen, but never expected to be taking part in a High Tea with Mr. Sherlock Holmes and Doctor Watson!"

"Indeed, you are doing no such thing, sir," Holmes said gently. "It is a common misconception, I gather, among our American cousins that High- and Afternoon- tea are the same thing. They are very different meals, taken at quite different times. High Tea was in my day only eaten at certain seats of learning, and was a hot, early supper. The same kind of supper, served in a nursery, has of late been known as High Tea. Afternoon-tea, which consists of a conventional cold sandwich selection, sometimes with scones, clotted cream and strawberry jam, is eaten by adults, generally at four o'clock. High Tea, by and large, is eaten by children at six o'clock. The sausage was always very evident at such meals when I was young." Holmes suppressed a subtle shudder.

"I stand corrected and instructed, sir," said the Texan jovially, and waved a delicate sandwich by way of emphasis. Whereupon all three of us broke into laughter — Holmes at his own pedantry and Mr. Macklesworth almost by way of relief from the weighty matters on his mind.

"Did you discover any clues to the mystery in High Cogges?" our guest wished to know.

"Oh, indeed, Mr. Macklesworth," said Holmes, "I have one or two things to verify, but think the case is solved." He chuckled again, this time at the expression of delighted astonishment on the American's face.

"Solved, Mr. Holmes?"

"Solved, Mr. Macklesworth, but not proven. Doctor Watson, as usual, contributed greatly to my deductions. It was you, Watson, who suggested the motive for involving this gentleman in what, I believe, was a frightful and utterly cold-blooded crime."

"So I was right, Mr. Holmes! Sir Geoffrey was murdered!"

"Murdered or driven to self-murder, Mr. Macklesworth, it is scarcely material."

"You know the culprit, sir?"

"I believe I do. Pray, Mr. Macklesworth," now Holmes pulled a piece of yellowed paper from an inner pocket, "would you look at this? I took it from my files on the way here and apologise for its somewhat dusty condition."

Frowning slightly, the Texan accepted the folded paper and then scratched his head in some puzzlement, reading aloud. *"My dear Holmes, Thank you so much for your generous assistance in the recent business concerning my young painter friend... Needless to say, I remain permanently in your debt. Yours very sincerely —"* He looked up in some confusion. "The notepaper is unfamiliar to me, Mr. Holmes. Doubtless the Athenaeum is one of your clubs. But the signature is false."

"I had an idea you might deduce that, sir," said Holmes, taking the paper from our guest. Far from being discommoded by the information, he seemed satisfied by it. I wondered how far back the roots of this crime were to be found. "Now, before I explain further, I feel a need to demonstrate something. I wonder if you would be good enough to write a note to Mrs. Gallibasta in Willesden. I would like you to tell her that you have changed your mind about returning to the United States and have decided to live in England for a time. Meanwhile, you intend to place the Fellini Silver in a bank vault until you go back to the United States, whereupon you are considering taking legal advice as to what to do with the statue."

"If I did that, Mr. Holmes, I would not be honouring my vow to my cousin. And I would be telling a lie to a lady."

"Believe me, Mr. Macklesworth if I assure you, with all emphasis, that you will not be breaking a promise to your cousin and you will not be telling a lie to a lady. Indeed, you will be doing Sir Geoffrey Macklesworth and, I hope, both our great nations, an important service."

"Very well, Mr. Holmes," said John Macklesworth, firming his jaw and adopting a serious expression, "if that's your word, I'm ready to go along with whatever you ask."

"Good man, Macklesworth!" Sherlock Holmes' lips drew back a little from his teeth, like a wolf scenting prey. "By the by, sir, have you ever heard of a creature known as 'Little Peter' or sometimes 'French Pete'?"

"Certainly I have, Mr. Holmes. He was a popular subject in the sensational press and remains so to this day. He operated out of New Orleans about a decade ago. Jean 'Petit Pierre' Fromental. He was part Creole, part Italian and, some said, part Cree. A powerful, handsome man who had been a Shakespearian actor, but was famous for a series of particularly vicious murders of well-known dignitaries in the private rooms of those establishments for which Picayune is famous. A woman accomplice was also involved. She was said to have lured the men to the rooms so that her paramour might kill them and rob them. Fromental was captured eventually but the woman was never arrested. Some believe it was she who helped him escape when he did. As I remember, Mr. Holmes, Fromental was never thereafter caught. There was a suggestion he went to Memphis and joined a travelling medicine show. Was there not some evidence that he, in turn, had been murdered by a woman? Do you think Fromental and Sir Geoffrey were both victims of the same murderess?"

"In a sense, Mr. Macklesworth. As I said, I am reluctant to give you my whole theory until I have put some of it to the test. But none of this is the work of a woman, that I can assure you. Will you do as I say?"

"Count on me, Mr. Holmes. I will compose the telegram now."

When Mr. Macklesworth had left our rooms, I turned to Holmes, hoping for a little further illumination, but he was nursing his solution to him as if it were a favourite child. The expression on his face was extremely irritating to me. "Come, Holmes, this won't do! You say I suggested the motive, yet you offer no hint of the solution! Mrs. Gallibasta is not the murderess, yet you say a murder is most likely involved. My theory — that Sir Geoffrey had the Silver spirited away and then killed himself so that he would not be committing a crime, as he would if he had been bankrupted — seems to confirm this. His handwriting has identified him as the author of the scheme. Now, suddenly, you speak of some Louisiana desperado known as 'Little Pierre', who appears to have been your main suspect until Mr. Macklesworth revealed that he was dead."

"I agree with you, Watson, that it seems very confusing. I hope for illumination tonight. Do you have your revolver with you, old friend?"

"I am not in the habit of carrying a gun about, Holmes."

At this, Sherlock Holmes crossed the room and produced a large shoe-box which he had also brought from 221b that afternoon. From it he produced two modern Webley revolvers and a box of ammunition. "We may need these to defend our lives, Watson. We are dealing with a master criminal intelligence. An intelligence both patient and calculating, who has planned this crime over many years and now believes there is some chance of being thwarted."

"You think Mrs. Gallibasta is in league with him and will warn him when the telegram arrives?"

"Let us say, Watson, that we must expect a visitor tonight. That is why the Fellini Silver stands in our window to be recognised."

I told my friend that at my age and station I was losing patience for this kind of charade, but reluctantly I agreed to accept the revolver and load it.

THE NIGHT WAS almost as sultry as the day and I was beginning to wish that I had availed myself of lighter clothing and a glass of water when I heard a strange, scraping noise from somewhere in the street and risked a glance down from where I stood in darkness behind the curtain.

I was astonished to see a figure, careless of any observer, yet fully visible in the yellow light of the lamps, climbing rapidly up the wisteria vine!

Within seconds the man — for man it was, and a gigantic individual, at that — had slipped a knife from his belt and was opening the catch on the window in which the Fellini Silver still sat. It was all I could do to hold my position. I could not speak, to warn Holmes, or our prey would bolt. Common sense told me he could not simply grab the Silver and leave. He would have to lower it by a rope or carry it down the stairs. This meant he had to enter the room where we awaited him.

The audacious burglar remained careless of any onlookers, as if his greed for the Silver so consumed him that he was oblivious to all ordinary considerations. I caught a glimpse of his features in the lamp-light. He had thick, wavy hair tied back in a bandanna, a couple of day's stubble on his chin and dark, almost negroid skin. I guessed at once that he was a relative of Mrs. Gallibasta.

Then he had snapped back the window catch and I heard his breath hissing from his lips as he raised the sash and slipped inside.

The next moment Holmes emerged from his hiding place and levelled the revolver at the man who turned with the blazing eyes of a trapped beast, knife in hand, his wild, dark eyes seeking escape.

"There is a loaded revolver levelled at your head, man," said Holmes evenly. "You would be wise to drop that knife and surrender — Jean-Pierre Fromental!"

With a wordless snarl, the intruder flung himself towards the Silver, placing it between himself and our guns.

He had a mad, careless expression upon his handsome features. "Shoot if you dare!" he cried. "You will be destroying more than my unworthy life! You will be destroying everything you have conspired to preserve! I underestimated you, Macklesworth, if that's you" — he gestured, in fact, towards me. "I thought you were an easy dupe — besotted by your belief that you were related to a knight of the realm, with whom you had an intimate correspondence! How readily you answered my questions! I worked for years to discover everything I could about you. You seemed perfect. You were willing to do anything, so long as it was described as a matter of family honour. Oh, how I planned! How I held myself in check! How patient I was! How noble in all my deeds! I ascertained you had no claim on the title or the estate, so would never need any contact with the executors. All so that I would one day own not merely that fool Geoffrey's money, but also his most prized treasure! I had his devotion — but I wanted everything else besides! And would have had it if you had not suddenly revealed a desire to stay in England!"

It was then, suddenly, that I understood the truth of the situation!

At that moment I saw a flash of silver and heard the sickening sound of steel entering flesh. With a sharp intake of breath, Holmes fell back, his pistol dropping from his hand. Yelling something incoherent, I fired my revolver, careless of Fellini or his art, fearing my friend was once again to be taken from me — this time before my eyes.

I saw Jean-Pierre Fromental, alias Linda Gallibasta, stagger backwards, arms raised, and then reach again towards the Fellini Silver
before losing balance and falling backwards, with a loud crash of
breaking glass and splintering timber, through the window. He
seemed to hover in the very air, supported by his will, his terrible
lust for the Fellini Silver, and then, with an animal cry, flail at the
air and fall, disappearing into a terrible, sudden silence.

At that moment, the door burst open and in came John
Macklesworth, closely followed by our old friend Inspector Lestrade,
Mrs. Ackroyd, and one or two other tenants of Number 2, Dorset
Street.

"It's all right, Watson," I heard Holmes say, a little faintly. "Only
a flesh wound. It was foolish of me not to know he could throw a
Bowie-knife! Get down there, Lestrade, and see what you can do.
I'd hoped to take him alive. It could be the only way we'll be able to
locate the money he has been stealing from his benefactor over all
these years. Good evening to you, Mr. Macklesworth. I had hoped
to convince you of my solution, but I had not expected to suffer
quite so much injury in the performance." His smile was faint and
his eyes were flooded with pain.

Luckily, I was able to reach my friend before he collapsed upon
my arm and allowed me to lead him to a chair, where I inspected
the wound. The knife had stuck in his shoulder and, as Holmes
knew, had done no permanent damage, but I did not envy him the
discomfort he was suffering.

Poor Macklesworth was completely stunned. His entire notion
of things had been turned topsy-turvy and he was having difficulty
taking everything in. After dressing Holmes's wound, I told
Macklesworth to sit down while I fetched everyone a brandy. Both
the American and myself were bursting to learn everything Holmes
had deduced, but contained ourselves until my friend would be in

better health. Now that the initial shock was over, however, he was in high spirits and greatly amused by our expressions.

"Your explanation was ingenious, Watson, and touched on the truth, but I fear it was not the answer. If you will kindly look in my inside jacket pocket, you will find two pieces of paper there. Would you be good enough to draw them out so that we might all see them?"

I did as my friend instructed. One was the last letter Sir Geoffrey had written to John Macklesworth and, ostensibly, left with Mrs. Gallibasta. The other, far older, was the letter John Macklesworth had read out earlier that day. Although there was a slight similarity to the hand-writing, they were clearly of different authorship.

"You said this was the forgery," said Holmes, holding up the letter in his left hand, "but unfortunately it was not. It is probably the only example of Sir Geoffrey's handwriting you have ever seen, Mr. Macklesworth."

"You mean he dictated everything to his — to that devil?"

"I fear, Mr. Macklesworth, that your namesake had never heard of your existence."

"He could not write to a man he had never heard of, Mr. Holmes!"

"Your correspondence, my dear sir, was not with Sir Geoffrey at all, but with the man who lies on the pavement down there. His name, as Doctor Watson has already deduced, is Jean-Pierre Fromental. No doubt he fled to England after the Picayune murders and, as an actor, easily got in with the likes of Frank Harris and the Bohemian crowd surrounding Lord Alfred Douglas, eventually finding exactly the kind of dupe he was looking for. It is possible he kept his persona of Linda Gallibasta all along. Certainly that would explain why he became so terrified at the thought of being examined by a doctor — you'll recall the postmistresses words. It is hard to know if he was permanently dressing as a woman — that, after all, is how he had lured his Louisiana victims to their deaths — and whether Sir Geoffrey knew much about him, but clearly he made himself invaluable to his employer and was able, bit by bit, to salt away the remains of the Macklesworth fortune. But what he really craved was the Fellini Silver, and that was when he determined the course of action which led to his calculating deception of you, Mr. Macklesworth. He needed a namesake living not far from New Orleans. As an added insurance he invented another cousin. By the simple device of writing to you on Sir Geoffrey's stationery he built up an entire series of lies, each of which had the appearance of verifying the other. Because, as Linda Gallibasta, he always collected the mail, Sir Geoffrey was never once aware of the deception."

It was John Macklesworth's turn to sit down suddenly as realisation dawned. "Good heavens, Mr. Holmes. Now I understand!"

"Fromental wanted the Fellini Silver. He became obsessed with the notion of owning it. But he knew that, if he stole it, there was little chance of his ever getting it out of the country. He needed a second dupe. That dupe was you, Mr. Macklesworth. I regret that you are probably not a very near cousin of the murdered man. Neither, I can assure you, did Sir Geoffrey fear for his Silver. He appeared quite reconciled to his poverty and had long since ensured that the Fellini Silver would remain in trust for his family or the public forever. In respect of the Silver he was sheltered from all debt by a special covenant with parliament. There was never a danger of the piece going to his creditors. There was, of course, no way in those circumstances that Fromental could get the Silver for himself. He had to engineer first a burglary — and then a murder, which looked like a consequence of that burglary. The suicide note was a forgery, but hard to decipher. His plan was to use your honesty and decency,

Mr. Macklesworth, to carry the Silver through to America. Then he planned to obtain it from you by any means he found necessary."

Macklesworth shuddered. "I am very glad I found you, Mr. Holmes. If I had not, by coincidence, chosen rooms in Dorset Street, I would even now be conspiring to further that villain's ends!"

"As, it seems, did Sir Geoffrey. For years he trusted Fromental. He appears to have doted on him, indeed. He was blind to the fact that his estate was being stripped of its remaining assets. He put everything down to his own bad judgement and thanked Fromental for helping him! Fromental had no difficulty, of course, in murdering Sir Geoffrey when the time came. It must have been hideously simple. That suicide note was the only forgery, as such, in the case, gentlemen. Unless, of course, you count the murderer himself."

John Macklesworth leapt to his feet. He strode forward with all the natural grace of the frontier gentleman and shook hands warmly with Sherlock Holmes. "I will be eternally grateful to you, Mr. Holmes. You have not only confirmed your reputation, but my common sense and good judgement! That is the best we can do for one another in this world, I believe. I can now spend a little time in your fine country and get to see all those romantic places I've only read about."

"I will be glad to recommend an itinerary!" I said, delighted and relieved by the turn of events. "And, indeed, if you enjoy fly fishing, it might be possible, dependant on a patient's condition, for me to show you a few little-known streams."

"Meanwhile," said Sherlock Holmes from his chair, "I must summon all my energy and ingenuity to find a good reason why Mrs. Hudson should not send me to recuperate at her sister's in Hove."

With a melancholy smile he asked me to pass him his cocaine and his syringe.

The End

And that was the end of the Dorset Street affair. The Fellini Silver was taken by the Victoria and Albert Museum who, for some years, kept it in the special 'Macklesworth' Wing before it was transferred, by agreement, to Sir John Soane's Museum. There the Macklesworth name lives on. John Macklesworth returned to America a poorer and wiser man. Fromental died in hospital, without revealing the whereabouts of his stolen fortune, but happily a bank book was found at Willesden and the money was distributed amongst Sir Geoffrey's creditors, so that the house did not have to be sold. It is now in the possession of a genuine Macklesworth cousin. Life soon settled back to normal and it was with some regret that we eventually left Dorset Street to take up residence again at 221b. I have occasion, even today, to pass that pleasant house and recall with a certain nostalgia the few days when it had been the focus of an extraordinary adventure and the scene of a thwarted crime...

HOW TOM MIX SAVED MY LIFE

I HAVE ALWAYS known, deep in my bones, that Tom Mix saved my life. I owe a singular confirmation of my nine-year-old instinct to Mrs. Helen Mullens of West Point, Mississippi. If it's possible to have a fairy mother-in-law on the lines of a fairy godmother, then she is it. This is not the first time she has helped me fulfil a dream or solve a mystery. She is also a Tom Mix fan.

After considerable searching and with the help of an old friend in Memphis, Tennessee, she brought to England last May a rare videotape of *My Pal, The King* (1930). For me, four empty decades were finally to be given meaning.

My Pal, The King isn't in Halliwell. You'd probably need some sort of specialist reference book to find it. The director rarely turns up in an index. Nonetheless I believe it has a small place in movie history. It marks the end of one substantial career and the beginning of another. With *Destry Rides Again* (1932) it was one of a handful of talking features made by Mix.

The film has the slight sense of incoherence peculiar to many pictures of the era, whose silent heroes had become a bit too old, slow and slurred for the transition. Hoot Gibson, Ken Maynard and Tim McCoy were all stronger when they were totally silent. Some, like Art Acord and Fred Thomson died young or hung up their saddles. Their films, which thrilled millions, are almost entirely lost. The heroes who had once done so many of their own stunts were now mere illusionists. Solutions to problems were provided by stand-ins, cut-aways, stuntmen and wonderful action footage, redubbed with pistol shots and so on, from their golden years.

Virtually every one of the cowboy stars had come up through the rodeos and began as stuntmen themselves. They had learned their trade. They could do all the standard riding, roping and shooting stunts which had been regular features of rodeos and Western shows for fifty years, from Guadalajara to Calgary.

According to Bret Harte, the French even had a name for these specialists. They called them *buflobils*. They had earned their wounds honourably. Like Mix, they had broken almost every bone at least once. Most of them signed lousy contracts and drank up their pay, just like the saddle bosses who had taught them their skills. They were usually hard up and the only way they knew to earn a living was to sit on a bronc and twirl a rope with one hand, while firing a pearl-handled Colt with the other. The harder it got, the more they had to drink. Histories of so many legendary cowboy stars ironically reflect the real, frequently tragic, stories of the Westerners they had helped mythologise.

They came to regard with amused bewilderment the rise of the sissified songsters in their diamante duds whose only skill was the ability to sit on a saddle on a wooden pony while moving their lips roughly in synch with the soundtrack. Like William S. Hart before them, they mourned the death of the old values. A few, such as Buck

Jones (whose posthumous scripts I once wrote) died genuinely he-roic deaths and cashed in their chips like true cowboys. Jones died when he repeatedly went back into the Coconut Grove to save people trapped in that famous Boston fire of 1942. Mix himself died in a car crash in 1940. Both Jones and John Wayne owed their early breaks to Mix. They also shared his values.

The silent stars left little behind them. Most of their films are brown dust and the few which remain are a record of daring action heroes performing in plots as rigid as the scenarios of the Wild West Shows they derived from. There is hardly any record remaining of their shows. Some of their talkies, usually in dilapidated prints, sur-vived, thanks mainly to the Saturday matinee audiences and their television equivalents. Almost always these are their worst work; bro-ken old men talking woodenly against painted backdrops.

With *My Pal, The King* Tom Mix left us something a little bit extra, including a detailed record of his Wild West Show and his straight-from-the-shoulder political testament. While the romance and the action were the original attraction, I now realise that Tom's message has stayed with me.

I couldn't tell you if I saw it first at the Norbury ABC, the Thornton Heath Granada, the Streatham Astoria or one of half a dozen other South London picture palaces. In those days rivalries existed between the various Saturday Morning Picture clubs, just as they did between supporters of Captain Marvel and Superman. I was prepared to suffer for my hero Captain Marvel, but as far as clubs were concerned, I knew no such loyalties. I could sing the ABC Mi-nor song as lustily as the Thornton Heath *Grenadiers*. On Saturday mornings I was prepared to travel from show to show to avoid the Three Stooges (who continue to leave me cold) or a Dagwood com-edy and find The Rocket Man or The Bowery Boys.

I think a fight broke out during *My Pal's* first bit of brief political exposition. I was close to the front and remember certain scenes where the noise level, coupled with the distortion from the speakers, made the plot more or less incomprehensible, and the slender rationalisations holding it together were lost to the distractions of licorice-all-sort fights and intense trading among the white mouse and cigarette card fancy.

In those days I knew Mickey Rooney far better than Tom Mix. *National Velvet* (1945) had been out for four years and on the SMP circuit Andy Hardy was a familiar, if not always welcome, face, but it could well have been the first time I'd seen Tom Mix.

What attracted me then, as now, to *My Pal, The King* was the peculiar blend of fairly disparate genre elements and its crystallised pulp plot. I've always had a relish for stuff like *The Phantom Empire*, a Gene Autry science-fiction Western serial, and the sequence in *Eagle* comic's first 'Dan Dare' serial, where United Nations mounted troops — household Cavalry, RCMPs, Arab spahis, Indian lancers, Texas cowboys, Cossacks etc. are landed by glider from spaceships orbiting Venus.

This is probably the only time the elements of *Prisoner of Zenda*-style fantasy, Western adventure, and direct, populist political message have ever been combined with valuable documentary footage from a more innocent past. The film is every bit as good as I remember. I found myself as thoroughly hooked as I had been the first time. I even cared what happened to Mickey Rooney.

Anyone with a relish for the odd byways of Hollywood should get a kick from *My Pal, The King*. It very directly offers us a reflection, in Mix's prolonged monologue, of the good-hearted American democratic idealism which at one time established a model for the rest of the world, but would go wrong with McCarthyism and Vietnam.

Mix speaks up for the rights of the individual, for the institutions and apparatus of democracy and how it makes plain sense to treat people like human beings, not brutes. It is well meaning and, if you like, naive. It is paternalistic (which is why it went sour) and it does rather echo George Bush's damaging triumphalism around the Gulf War, but at root it contains a message which has to do with self-respect and human rights. I find little wrong with the sentiments. They were pretty much the same ones which powered the New Deal and produced the regenerated America it took Wayne's pard Ronald Reagan to dismantle in the name of liberty. One old-timer's crackerbarrel, I guess, is another's tub of poisoned jerky.

The film was produced by Carl Laemmle and directed by Kurt Neumann. When it was made, Mix had been persuaded by Universal to try a come-back. Mix, like several others, had returned to the road with his Wild West Show. Dozens of accidents had left him stiff and almost crippled and about all he could do himself were a few basic roping and shooting tricks.

Somebody at Universal decided to take advantage of the situation and produced a story in which Tom, as a rodeo boss, goes with his show to Europe. Mickey Rooney, as Charles the boy king of a Balkan nation not a stone's throw from Ruritania, is bored by politics. Villainous aristocrats plan to use the boy for their own ends and introduce dictatorship to Malvonia. It's at this point that the cowboys and Indians come to town. Young King Charles sneaks off to see the parade, meets Mix and introduces the ruggedly arthritic buckaroo to the lovely Princess Elsa (Noel Francis). All this happens in the first few minutes.

Suspicious of Tom's easy-going democratic small-talk, the tyrannical Count de Mar (James Kirkwood) resists the boy's enthusiasm, but eventually, with his kindly mentor Professor Lorenz (Wallis Clark), Charles gets to go to the show.

What follows is pretty much the whole of Mix's show, evidently filmed by a different hand, inserted piecemeal into the movie. Cows are wrestled, broncs are bucked and Indians attack a racing stagecoach. At the end of it all Tom and King Charles sit together in the royal throne room and discuss the fundamental business of the pursuit of life, liberty and happiness for all, in exactly those words.

When Tom asks the king what he plans to do when he grows up, Charles says miserably that he guesses he'll collect his share of the taxes and have a good time.

"Hey, buddy — somebody's bin givin' yuh the wrong advice," says Tom in deep concern.

The king asks him what he'd do.

Tom says he'd run a fair sorta government. "I'd take th' people's taxes an' build parks, schoolhouses, hospitals, roads, public playgrounds. Yes, sir, that's what I'd do. Treat everybody right."

King Charles is converted. "That's a wonderful idea, Tom. I'll do it."

"Then you'll be admired an' respected an' they wouldn't be runnin' around huntin' yuh up with a bomb in their hands," Tom opines wisely.

This kind of red republicanism incenses Count de Mar and when, fired by Tom's democratic ideals, King Charles refuses to sign certain documents, the Count resorts to more direct methods of control. Consequently, King Charles is abducted to a castle where the vicious Count offers Charles' mentor, Professor Lorenz, the opportunity to kill himself and the boy with a revolver or threatens to sentence them both to be killed by the leering gaoler, Eizel, in some hideously prolonged fashion.

Meanwhile, excusing himself from his ongoing romance with Princess Elsa, Tom gets on the boy's trail. His posse of buckaroos,

gauchos, redskins and rodeo clowns rides to rescue the king. Ultimately they realise they must storm the castle.

Eat your heart out, young Rassendyll. Malvonia's must be the only medieval castle in Europe to be attacked by whooping Sioux, hollering cowboys, trick-shooting vaqueros, bolas-whirling gauchos and equestrian augustes. With their rodeo and circus skills to aid them, they succeed in entering the castle and help Tom save King Charles as he is moments from drowning.

An epilogue shows Tom bidding farewell to his sighing sweetheart and downcast Rooney. Reminding the boy of his democratic destiny and with an assurance from Charles that those values will now inform every aspect of Malvonian life, Tom takes a cowpoke's farewell. A tip of his hat and he is, almost for the last time, swallowed by the sunset.

It is a very satisfactory resolution. All evil is banished. Virtue triumphs. Heroism is recognised and courage rewarded; a secure future lies ahead and a clear message is delivered to tyrants everywhere. You can almost hear Will Rogers spitting reflectively over the hitching rail and drawling, "An' this means you, Sig-nor Musso-leeni!"

I grew up, with Jewish ancestors, in V-bombed London. It was young Americans inspired by those simple ideals who turned up to save me in the nick of time. If they hadn't, I'd probably be dead.

Maybe that idealism later turned sour because it wouldn't translate into simple solutions. But I'm in no doubt whatsoever about its importance to me.

Michael Moorcock
Queens Club Gardens,
London, June 1993

A CATALOGUE OF MEMORIES
The Family Library Vol. XVII. No. VII

B ooks selected from the Family Library of the Moorcocks of Tower House, Moorcock, Nr. Dent, Wensleydale, N. Yorkshire. Chiefly representative of Sir Arthur Moorcock's (b. 1912) taste for rare and unusual memoirs and records. Published with his permission and that of the present incumbent who compiled the selection.

(Note: This Catalogue is only a partial version of the original which was lost in the Tower House fire of 1996.)

ARKWRIGHT-BEGG, Q.T.
The Weather in London, A Memoir of Droving Days. Lindsay & McLellan, Sydney, 1904. First Edition. With illustrations by the Author. 346pp, Doct, Half-Calf.

This is the true first edition beginning with CHAPTER ONE: "The Australian Outback, though generally pretty inhospitable, has provided me with some of the most magical sights of my life. I have witnessed the great red and black sun rising over the yum-yum trees

while a flight of vividly coloured berry birds formed an almost perfect pentagram against the yellow sky. I have seen the Lost Inland
Sea and the Katata Play and I have explored Moo-Uria, where all
our ancestors came from and where the so-called 'Offmoo'
civilisation has achieved a balanced perfection." (This is missing from
the English and subsequent editions. The Author died soon after
publication and his family insisted on the excisions and revisions).

AARON. J. M.
*East End/West End: Life on the Border. Growing Up In Brookgate
before the War.* Camden Public Libraries, London, 1969. Paper
covers.

Jack Aaron was a well known journalist in the 1950s, covering
the Malayan campaigns for the *Telegraph* and resigning when stories
of British brutality went unpublished by the paper. He later became
bureau chief of UPF until 1974 when he died suddenly. M. J.
Moorcock worked with him in the 1960s when Aaron was develop-
ing *ABROAD* magazine for Amalgamated Press and Moorcock was
freelancing. Aaron's pamphlet is an unsentimental record of hard
times, of running a stall in Old Sweden Street market and attending
the famous 'Ragged University' run by Professor Marcus Wells under the Farringdon Road arches (and later in Smithfield). The pub-
licity the pamphlet received at the time of its publication concerned
a passing reference to the homosexual activities of two members of
the Royal Family in Brookgate during the 1930s.

BALLARD. Dr. J.D.
The Geometries of the Natural World. Blackwell's, Oxford, 1928.
1st Printing. Diagrams by the Author. 210pp. Qto. Red boards.

One of three known proof copies not destroyed after the police
seizure of October 1928. This contains the suppressed pages beginning: "At dawn, when the wild flamingoes congregated in the

swampy shallows, Trellis would go down to the shore and stare for hours at the reeds and water, noting the eccentric alphabets and uneven geometries of the lagoons. At these moments he would recall the time when he, J.K., J.O., P.M. and M.M. had exchanged underwear during a bus trip to Washington in the summer of 1960." In this same peculiar book, part-reminiscence, part-philosophy, part prediction, the Author describes a landing on the Moon by a robot plane and reveals an obsession with personalities who would not be famous until the 1950s and 1960s.

BEK, Count Dorian von ('Ali Mohamet').
My Days in the Desert. Ludwig Holt, New York, 1915. 1st edition. Photographs by the Author. 302pp. Doct. Green boards.

The story of the Fahazid Wars of the Mauretanian Succession in the '90s and Count von Bek's considerable involvement. He was said to have the ear of the Caliph. 'Indeed,' claimed one Englishman, 'and he'd have had the nose and foreskin, too, if the poor bugger still possessed either.' Von Bek built what was virtually a miniature empire in the NW Sahara and for a while was considered a serious threat by the Great Powers, to be treated with, rather than threatened. He died in 1932, leading a squadron of irregular Rif cavalry against the Spanish Foreign Legion at the Battle of Meknes.

BEK, Baroness Tabatha.
Ferret Dawn. A Highland Romance. Sidgwick & Jackson, London, 1956. Drawings by the Author. 220pp. Decorated boards and d/w by Biro.

Lady Tabatha Bek was active in Labour Party politics immediately after the 2nd World War. She was the first Chairwoman of the NCB and actively involved in the creation of the MMB and EMB. She held various ministerial posts before retiring to the Highlands to breed ferrets. The sudden disappearance of her husband in 1961 was reported widely in the press, but he was never found. Lady Tabatha disappeared two years later, apparently while walking with her weasels on the beach near her home on Skye.

SWORD OF IRONY

An Introduction to Fritz Leiber's Grey Mouser stories

CELE GOLDSMITH (later Lalle) is one of the great editors of science fantasy and, with Judith Merrill, godmother to the American sf New Wave of the 1960's. She published all the Young Turks, most of them for the first time, in the magazines she edited — the venerable *FANTASTIC STORIES* and *AMAZING STORIES,* two of the oldest specialised pulps in print.

Lalle had a liking for what one of her contributors had christened 'Sword and Sorcery' and she commissioned a young John Jakes to write her a series of Conan-like adventures, *Brak the Barbarian.* She published an early fantasy of mine called *Earl Aubec and the Golem,* which she retitled *Master of Chaos.* She published the first Roger Zelazny story — and published many more. She published Thomas M. Disch and J. G. Ballard and Samuel R. Delany and all the exciting talents which helped create that wonderful sea-change of the 1960's. She also liked Philip K. Dick and Keith Laumer, but I think her favourite writer, whose talent stood so far above the majority of his more financially successful peers, was Fritz Leiber.

Like so many of us, Cele Goldsmith treasured the handful of stories which Leiber (pronounced, if someone hasn't already mentioned this, in the original German fashion — as Lie-ber — Fritz could be sensitive about that) had published in John W. Campbell's much-loved fantasy magazine *UNKNOWN*. These included *Adept's Gambit* and the others which appeared in a small press edition in 1947 called *Two Sought Adventure*. Those of us lucky to have a copy treasured it in common with our rare editions of Dunsany and Morris. Leiber was perceived as a writer of literary adventure fantasy, a stylist with the same delicacy of touch that marked Stevenson or Chesterton, a modern (and, some thought, superior) James Branch Cabell.

In those days the kind of supernatural romance which dominates today's best-seller lists had virtually no commercial market. Leiber had done no better with his first Gray Mouser book than I had done with my first Elric book. Not only publishers scoffed at the notion of mass market editions of these books, we authors scoffed equally. We knew there were only about twenty of us — readers and writers — spread thin across Britain and America... So Cele Goldsmith, when she commissioned Fritz Leiber to write a new series of Fafhrd and Gray Mouser stories for *FANTASTIC*, was taking a big gamble with her circulation figures.

As Merrill did with her opinion-moulding *Year's Best SF Stories*, Goldsmith had to create a climate for the kind of fiction she enjoyed. J. R. R. Tolkien was still an obscure academic who had published a peculiar trilogy with a William Morris/Anglo Saxon ring to it and had yet to become the core of a somewhat unhealthy cult.

Few recognised the tradition in which we wrote and the public for our work numbered a few thousand throughout the world. The works of most of our predecessors — whether commercial writers like Howard, Burroughs and Merritt or literary writers like Dunsany and Cabell — were largely out of print and hard to find. If Goldsmith had been a modern editor, she would have known that statistically she could not publish such fiction and would have followed commercial wisdom by buying stories which were exactly like all the other stories she was publishing.

But, happily, Goldsmith was an old-fashioned editor willing to back her tastes and instincts with her own job and the circulations of the magazines she produced for Ziff Davis. Like Merrill, she preferred to publish what was good and frequently off-beat rather than what was safe. And, not surprisingly, her circulation figures improved...

If Goldsmith had been a 1990's corporate editor, the majority of Fritz Leiber's outstanding Mouser/Fafhrd would never have appeared. Modern American heroic fantasy could be said to owe its existence chiefly to her efforts and the enthusiasms of Donald A. Wollheim who discovered a loophole in the copyright law and brought out an unauthorized mass market edition of *The Lord of the Rings* — discovered that by an oversight Edgar Rice Burroughs's *A Princess of Mars* was out of copyright and published that. Together — and a little later with Lynn Carter's programme of classic (public domain) reprints for Ballantine — they launched what has now become the dominant genre in modern fantastic fiction.

Meanwhile the Young Turks, given a public by Lalle and Merrill, rejecting their immediate predecessors as Young Turks will, were all agreed that there were two writers of the earlier generation whose literary standards and skills, whose talent and sensibility they still admired and envied. One was Philip K. Dick. The other was Fritz

Leiber, whose masterly prose and urbane wit continued to outshine our callow talents. We revered him. We still do.

Fritz Leiber Jr., son of the (at one time) more famous Fritz Leiber Sr., had the benefit of a good, old-fashioned education, a thorough reading in the classics, a casual knowledge of Shakespeare and a relish for oratory inherited from his father. Fritz Leiber Sr. was a very famous Shakespearian stage actor who occasionally appeared in films, much as Alec Guinness pops up in *Star Wars*, to give them a bit of class. The Leiber profile was familiar to pre-war audiences, both in silent epics and in talkies. Anyone who has seen *Captain Blood* will remember Fritz Sr. as Judge Jeffreys in the tremendous court-room scene designed by Anton Grot, and anyone who has seen *Camille* will remember Fritz Jr. as Robert Taylor's handsome friend.

In short, while he loved the stories he read in WEIRD TALES, supernatural fiction was not his only reading and his experience and expectations of the world were greater, far more sophisticated and more varied than those, say, of Lovecraft or Clark Ashton Smith, whom he enjoyed. His own literary skills were generally far better than the majority of writers he admired and, because he had read so widely and with such relish, his ambitions, his standards were considerably higher than most of the excellent writers who appeared beside him in *UNKNOWN, GALAXY* or *FANTASTIC STORIES OF THE IMAGINATION*. I once asked him why he wrote for commercial magazines whose audiences sometimes actively disliked his best work. He said that in the late 30's and 40's writers like himself — and he named Robert Bloch and Henry Kuttner amongst them — had no market at all, if they didn't have the pulp sf market. The literary market simply wasn't interested in their 'surrealist' fantasies. So they adapted them to the pulp market and earned a little money while they learned.

Ultimately, Fritz admitted, one found oneself getting increasingly interested in the genre for its own sake. Fritz, together with a handful of other fine writers of his generation, was one of those who helped create the literary conventions which exist in all popular science fiction today, from *Star Trek* to *Blade Runner*.

It became a familiar refrain, amongst Leiber enthusiasts, that he was too good for his markets and that he was ahead of his time. Both these things were to some extent true — the markets of those days were far less sophisticated than those of today and a lot of sf readers — who made up the majority in an extremely small market — were deeply conservative, actively disliking anything which was not the 'hard' sf of the kind appearing in *ASTOUNDING* (later *ANALOG*) and believing Sword and Sorcery to be an illogical and unwholesome abomination. Amongst the horror fans, any form of humour was regarded almost as blasphemy.

UNKNOWN, which specialised in fine humorous fantasy, including the Harold Shea stories of L. Sprague de Camp and *The Compleat Werewolf* stories of Anthony Boucher, had never been a great commercial success. Its taste was regarded as being that of a relatively small elite. Leiber's science fiction, such as his classic *Gather, Darkness!*, in which he cleverly rationalised the same images he was using in his fantasy, was far more successful. For a long time he wrote mostly sf, much of it highly original and seminal in its influence, some of it baffling to audiences of the day. He could not help himself. He was innovative, he was a writer with a lot of ideas he wanted to explore, in as many ways as he could, and a glance through his collected short stories will tell you how well he could write in many different forms.

Judith Merrill, a great supporter of Leiber's work, used to reckon that it took the public twenty years to catch up with Fritz. But being pretty much always twenty years ahead of his time and, it should be admitted, inclined to drink his profits rather than put them in a savings account, Fritz managed to die with too much of his best work unavailable to the general reader.

I've never forgotten a particular trip to New York in the mid-1960's. Four of us had driven in from the country. Merrill, a native New Yorker, refused to drive in the city. I had no licence and Jim Sallis (author of *Moth* and other fine thrillers) who had never driven in New York before was the only one of us capable of driving. Three of us sat in the front and the back seat was given over to Fritz who lay sprawled and fairly stoned reciting *Lepanto* by G. K. Chesterton in all its many verses in his deep, massive, stage-trained voice.

Suddenly Jim, who was horribly underslept, stopped the car in the middle of the street and announced that he refused to drive any further. We were in the middle of Sixth Avenue traffic at four o'clock in the afternoon on an August week-day and the traffic around us was not at one with itself. We rapidly (and fairly) became the chief focus of its disapproval. At Judy's insistence, Fritz was brought down to about five feet above ground level and told to drive. Without missing a verse, Fritz climbed behind the wheel and flew us with graceful panache to our destination (don't try this at home, children). Until it deteriorated beyond recovery, I had a tape of *Lepanto* which Fritz had made for me to remind me of that occasion. He could be a generous, extravagant soul and his relish for life comes out in particular in these wonderful stories.

Fritz, amongst others, has told the story of how the little Mouser and the burly Fafhrd were created — almost as people these days create role-playing worlds for their own pleasure — by himself and his friend Harry Otto Fischer, who wrote ten thousand words of the original story. These stories were never written to make money. Indeed, just as I did with my Elric stories of the early 60's, Fritz always considered them chiefly a labour of love, written for the pleasure of the telling, the delight in his characters and their wonderfully original world of Nehwon.

Cele Goldsmith's enthusiasm had encouraged Fritz to write the stories for her magazine, but Fritz did not really expect them to appear in book form. And then Donald A. Wollheim, that extraordinary and indefatigable catalyst, commissioned him to turn them into the series of novels now being so deservedly republished. The fantasy genre owes those two editors an enormous debt. Perhaps because they worked mostly as pulp fiction editors, they have never been given the considerable credit they deserve, just as Fritz himself — who wrote so much that was illuminating on the subject of literary fantasy and who wrote some of the best examples there will ever be — still does not receive sufficient credit for his enormous contribution to the genre. The publication of these volumes by White Wolf should do much to help remind readers of fantasy of their debt to a writer who is, in my opinion, still the greatest of us all.

Michael Moorcock
Lost Pines,
Texas
May 1995

THE SUN OF ITS PARTS
A Review of
The Arabian Nights: A Companion
Robert Irwin
Allen Lane: The Penguin Press, £20

WHEN I WORKED in the folk-hero industry, on Tarzan, Buffalo Bill, Jet Ace Logan, Robin Hood, Dick Turpin, Sexton Blake and others, some readers believed all those heroes to be real. So stylised were most of our scenarios that when original story cycles and legend combined with some new notion, it could spontaneously produce fresh conventions and enduring themes. The original evidence Robert Irwin presents in his marvellous, scholarly book shows that genre fiction has always been created in this way.

Whether in Marrakech or Wapping, storytellers working for a day's pay in the day's market learn to do it fast, do it good and do it often. They must be expert judges of how much fantasy and invention the market will bear (certain themes of sex, power and violence are always popular). They combine any new ideas with standard plots to keep the reader interested; they adapt them to the taste of the day. A talented author can improve a series or a genre beyond recognition. But it is largely an anonymous industry, where failing to keep your readers' immediate attention soon loses you your living.

Newspaper editors, too, must think up fresh combinations or, come the dawn, their heads will roll. The violence of proprietors has grown marginally less lethal, but otherwise not a lot has changed since Sheherazade determined to keep her sultan's bum on his seat and her own head on her shoulders. Every writer's unofficial patron saint, she is a model to us all and the envy of most.

The development and sophistication of that vast, mysterious Arabian miscellany — first partially translated from an Egyptian-Syrian manuscript by Galland in 1704 and from his French into English in 1708 — is in itself a fascinating story. The *Nights* existed in cruder versions (sans Sheherazade) from about the ninth century A.D. and translations from the Arabic (themselves often from other oriental sources) had begun to appear in Europe, as Irwin's excellent chronology and bibliography show, with the Spanish *Sindibad* in 1283, the year the Tunisian pornographer Al-Tayfashi died in Cairo. Once translated, the stories had a huge immediate impact on European letters.

The great Moorish/European/Ottoman cross-fertilisation never ceased. Irwin shows how Ali Baba himself, still an Arab TV hero, might actually be a French creation. From the beginning, Christendom and Islam profoundly influenced each other. Literature owes almost as much to *The Arabian Nights* as science to algebra, astronomy and alchemy. Styles and theories go in and out of fashion, but stories rarely do.

Literary tastes changed as radically in Baghdad as in Paris or Peking. The *Nights* reflects periods of license, when outright pornography was tolerated, periods of prurience, of high asceticism, of euphuism and baroque romanticism. In the various versions of the manuscript (none earlier than the Mamluke Syrian text used by Galland) the internal moral emphasis can change as much as the style. Homosexual love is therefore both celebrated and castigated in the same collection.

Barely able to write my own name in Arabic, I am awed by Irwin's achievement. The translator of "Middle Arabic" is faced with an often ambiguously rendered lexicon, rich in subtleties and crucial nuances, a rather short supply of good tools (no Arab equivalent of the OED) and a literature delighting in puns and word-plays where understanding depends on the individual intelligence, scholarship, talent, judgement and even humour of the translator. Inevitably, any translation from Arabic significantly reflects the medium, which is why there can be no "translation" of the Koran, only a "companion."

Irwin organises his material like a good story-teller. By cramming his Tardis of a book with tales of the tragic and comic, ironic and sentimental, lascivious and uplifting, commonplace and magical, with categories including sex and SF, Irwin escapes the problems of literal translation, literary taste or popular fashion and gives us the crystallised sum of the *Nights*: anecdote, history, moral fable, aphorism, story after story, wonder upon wonder. This monumental, infinitely faceted gem should be every writer's bedtime sampler.

In their western versions, the *Nights* are simply a further stage in a natural process of translation and retranslation, discovery and rediscovery, or decline and development. Much remains only in its original, almost untranslatable to this day, and little (including

Burton's porned-up misogynist version) is faithful to any original manuscript. Those who accuse Disney of "westernising" *Aladdin* didn't know, for instance, that he too was probably a French bastard. But maybe not — the *Nights* has attracted some first-rate forgers.

When I wrote popular stories, people thought our fictitious characters were real. Today, real lives are systematically fictionalised for popular consumption, a process which while not new has rarely been practised with such lazy profligacy. Still, the banal old story of *Diana and Charles* will have to perk up a lot before it will ever rival the altogether more Rabelaisian and entertaining tale of Princess Budur and Prince Kamar al-Zaman. While extolling the virtues of love between men, Budur (dressed as a boy) offers to bugger her paramour. The rest you will have to read for yourself . . .

MY COMIC LIFE

M Y CAREER IN COMICS began in 1956 when I began contributing to the national juvenile magazine TARZAN ADVENTURES, a weekly containing both text and strips. I wrote articles, stories and the text of a Hal Foster Tarzan series whose English plates had been destroyed in the Blitz. Most of my early strips can be identified by the use of well-known sf people of the time — Greg Benford and his brother Jim, for instance. I became editor of TARZAN in 1957. By 1959 I was on the staff of Fleetway's SEXTON BLAKE LIBRARY, also putting together annuals, like the KIT CARSON COWBOY ANNUAL, ROBIN HOOD ANNUAL, BILLY THE KID ANNUAL and sometimes LION and TIGER annuals. These were the hard-bound Christmas versions of the weeklies and monthlies I also came to work on. I edited issues of Thriller Picture Library, Cowboy Picture Library, and others. Apart from work for the annuals (usually one-off specials of other people's characters, like Karl the Viking which I did with Don Lawrence) I worked primarily for the monthly digest-sized comics. I wrote quite a few Kit Carson and Buck Jones adventures, Dick Daring of the Mounties, historical and other non-fiction pictorial features, and helped create Dogfight Dixon RFC, for which I did some of my most elaborate scripts. I started working for the weeklies chiefly as a freelance. I specialised in educational stuff, though I wrote a lot of adventure strips of all kinds. I worked for LOOK AND LEARN (*The Life of Alexander* with Don Lawrence), LION (Skid Solo), TIGER (Zip Nolan, Highway Patrol), BOYS WORLD (What Would You Do? Would You Believe It?) and the very lucrative BIBLE STORY WEEKLY (Constantine, The First Christian Emperor, with Don Lawrence). Contrary to popular opinion, I never wrote any episodes of WRATH OF THE GODS, DEATHWORLD or THE TRIGAN EMPIRE. By 1965 I had pretty much stopped writing comics and did nothing until I wrote the Jerry Cornelius strip, in collaboration with others, for *International Times* in 1969/70. In the early seventies, with Jim Cawthorn, I did a story-line for an Elric-meets-Conan story by Barry Windsor-Smith. This was written by Roy Thomas who would adapt my own Elric books so well for Pacific Comics and later for First Comics. In the late 70's, after quite a few versions of my characters had been done by various artists, I did my first new story with Howard Chaykin, for whom I had considerable admiration. *The Swords of Heaven, The Flowers of Hell* functions as an independent tale of The Eternal Champion and has a legitimate place in the sequence. My interest in comics freshened again with the advent of ambitious writers like Alan Moore and Neil Gaiman, writer-artists like Bryan Talbot and others. I did not follow the increasing maturity and ambition of graphic fiction at every stage, but it was clear its aspirations were growing and it was finding the techniques to match the aspirations. Even then, I felt no strong urge to write for this medium.

Eventually, in 1996, after I had been looking at a batch of current comics and realised what kind of ideas were now common currency, I suddenly felt like writing comics again. Through a couple of coincidences I was in touch with DC. Mike Friedrich proposed Michael Moorcock's Multiverse and DC liked the idea. I'll be working on three stories an issue — the first with Walter Simonson, the second with Mark Reeve and the third with John Ridgway — all of which will interweave and become part of one story. They are respectively Moonbeams and Roses (Simonson), The Metatemporal Detective (Reeve), and Duke Elric (Ridgway). The backgrounds and many of the characters are drawn from my Second Ether stories *Blood, Fabulous Harbours* and *The War Amongst the Angels.*

JOHNNY LONESOME
COMES TO TOWN
A Tale of the Far West

WHEN Johnny Lonesome rode into Shining Sands, Arizona, he wasn't looking for trouble. But trouble, it seemed, was looking for Johnny. Lots of trouble.

The young wandering cowboy knew that the Apaches had hit the war-trail again, so when he reined in his horse outside the sheriff's office, he expected bad news.

As Johnny entered his office, sheriff Bart Dawson pushed back his chair, got up, and stuck out a brawny hand in Johnny's direction.

"Howdy, Johnny," he grinned, "It's been a long time."

Lonesome gripped the big fist, "Too long," he smiled back. "How're things in your territory, Bart?"

The sheriff pointed a thumb towards the two iron-barred cells behind him. "Bad, Johnny. Apache outbreaks all over the country."

The cells were occupied by three scowling Apache braves, still in war-paint.

"War Lance, again?" asked Johnny.

"Yep! He says white men have been stealin' his hosses — and he wants revenge. Three ranches have been burned to the ground already! This bunch of rattlesnakes belong to War Lance's band — we caught 'em tryin' to raid a stage."

"Have you sent anyone out to War Lance's camp to arrange peace-talks?" Johnny sat down, his spurs jingling.

"Sent a deputy up there — got his scalp back yesterday."

Johnny was stopped from saying anything more by the sudden and noisy arrival of a tired-looking cowpoke who burst into the office. The man was covered in trail-dust and had obviously been riding hard.

"Sheriff Dawson — I'm from Merikville – we've had an outbreak of typhus down there and can't do a thing about it. It's spreadin' like a prairie fire! We heard your doctor's got some new kind o' drug that'll cure typhus fever — is that so?"

"Yep! That's right, son — Doc Weir got a shipment of some drug from back East which is reckoned to cure typhus. You'd better get straight over to his office and tell him what's happened." Dawson turned to Johnny. "You know where Doc Weir's office is, don't you, Johnny? Maybe you could show this hombre where it is?"

"Be glad to, Bart. I'm on my way!" Johnny led the dusty cowpoke out of the office and down the street.

"Any idea how this fever started?" he asked the man as they walked towards Doc Weir's surgery.

"That's what's worryin' our Doc in Merikville," replied the cowpoke, wiping a stained bandana across his grimy face. "He's looked for the source everywhere — but as far as he can see, it just ain't in Merikville!"

They reached the doctor's office and Johnny rapped loudly on the door. "Open up, Doc! This is Johnny Lonesome an' it's an emergency!"

"It's always an emergency o' some kind when that ornery varmint comes to town!" grumbled a good-humoured voice on the other side of the door. It was swung open and a little man of fifty or fifty-five stood looking up at Johnny's rugged face. His eyes sparkled. "How are yuh, Johnny, yuh no good son-of-a-gun? What's the trouble? More Apache arrow-wounds?"

"I'm fine, Doc, but the trouble's nothing to do with Apaches for once. This hombre wants to see you. He's ridden all the way from Merikville. Seems they got a typhus germ running around over there."

"Typhus! Well, well — that's bad, but it's lucky I sent back East when I did. Heard about this new drug and got some of it. I'll dig some of it out and let yuh have it pronto!"

Doc Weir disappeared, leaving Johnny and the cowpoke at the door. Johnny took off his stetson and entered the surgery.

The Doc was back almost within seconds. In his hands was a paper-wrapped packet. "Here yuh are, Johnny. The directions about how t'use it are inside. You'd better take it back to Merikville right away. This gent looks so tired I guess if he rides another mile I'll get him back as a patient. Good luck, Johnny – and watch out for Apaches — there's a lot of 'em in these parts right now!"

"I'll do my best to keep my hair fixed to my head!" grinned Johnny, "So long, Doc — I'll be seeing you!"

Apache Attack!

The hot Arizona sun beat down mercilessly as Johnny urged his horse across the barren plains towards Merikville. To the East he could see the Deathshead Mountains where War Lance's almost invincible camp was hidden; to the West was stretch after stretch of dry soil — and beyond it, the sand of the Arizona Desert.

Johnny's tongue was dry in his mouth as he rode, and his throat was parched. Yet there was no time to stop for water — a few minutes' delay might mean unnecessary suffering for the victims of the typhoid fever in Merikville.

"Half-way there, old hoss," he whispered to his speeding mount as he leaned low in the saddle, shielding his face as best he could from the stinging trail-dust.

He looked eastwards, towards the mountains and the words caught in his throat. A small dust-cloud was visible, coming nearer. It could only mean one thing — Apaches!

Johnny knew there was nothing to do but keep riding and hope to reach Merikville before the Apache war-party caught up with him. But in his heart he knew he wouldn't make it. He was going to have to fight it out – and every moment lost might mean death to a citizen of Merikville!

The dust-cloud came nearer and now Johnny could see the Indians. Their savage faces were painted in vivid war-paint and they waved gleaming Winchester carbines and Sharps repeaters. Johnny got his own Winchester 73 out of his saddle-boot and levered a shell into the breach.

The Apaches came nearer and Johnny turned in the saddle, drawing a bead on the nearest redskin rider.

The Winchester barked once and flamed death. The Apache dropped from his pony and his companions barely managed to stop their own ponies from riding over his body. Johnny saw that there were four of them now. Four Apaches coming closer all the time.

The young cowboy looked ahead and saw rocks looming towards him. They'd offer cover, but they were also going to slow him down.

He turned in his saddle again and sent another shot behind him. He could hear the triumphant war cries of the party and bullets began to whistle around him. A shell tugged at his shirt-sleeve and grazed his arm.

Johnny slid his six-shooter from its holster now that the range had decreased. He fired twice and saw another Apache go down. The remaining three braves still came on.

He reached the rocks and his horse struggled to keep a footing on them. They were wet and slippery. It was too late when Johnny saw the water below him. The stallion slipped, tried to right its fall and then went tumbling down towards the water below.

Somehow Johnny kept his seat as the big horse hit the water. Miraculously he managed to guide his mount so that it hit smoothly. Above him, the Apache braves had reached the rocks. Bullets hummed like hornets around Johnny's head as he urged his horse to swim to the opposite bank of the small lake.

He looked back. The Apaches were still firing at him but their own unshod ponies refused to make the descent towards the lake.

Johnny grinned, the lake had done him some good, after all.

His horse struggled from the water and galloped on towards Merikville. "We needed a drink anyway, old hoss," said Johnny cheerfully as his eyes made out the roofs of the town ahead of him.

* * *

Doctor Raveer stroked his small goatee beard worriedly as he took the package. "Thanks Johnny," he said, "We'll be able to save all the citizens of this town but it's a mystery to me how it started. There's no resident who could have passed it on and the water is untainted. I guess that there's a typhus carrier loose in this territory."

"A typhus *carrier* – what's that, Doc?" Johnny had never heard of such a thing before.

"Well, it seems that the big doctors back east, apart from inventing a drug which cures typhus, have discovered that it's possible for a man or woman to carry the typhus germs in their bodies — without actually having typhoid fever themselves! Instead they pass it on to other people, who get it. Generally these 'carriers' don't know they are what they are, so it's not their faults. I guess that's what happened in this case..."

"Well, I guess I'm in no danger from this 'carrier,' Doc. I've already had typhus. I think I'll see if I can find out who the carrier is — if he's riding towards Shining Sands, we might get another outbreak there!"

"I'd be grateful if you could, Johnny. The sooner that character's found the better. What with the Apaches raiding the territory and half the townships down with fever, we wouldn't stand a chance. Somebody's *got* to find that carrier, Johnny, and *fast!*"

The Horse Dealer

Johnny spent a couple of hours enquiring around Merikville. He wanted to know if anyone had recently passed through the town without staying for long. Eventually he was lucky — Slim Mercer the blacksmith knew of someone.

"Reckon I can guess who the man you're lookin' fer is, Johnny. Hombre name of Carl Knox. He's a horse-dealer. Knox sold a bunch of half-wild, unshod horses to Luke Wade, the rancher. He had supper with Wade and then rode on — seemed in a powerful hurry. Reason I know about him is that I shod the horses for Wade last night — Wade himself told me — before he went down with typhus!"

"That sounds like my man!" Johnny rubbed his chin thoughtfully, "How long a start would you say he'd got on me, Slim?"

"A good day's ride — maybe more. But I know one thing — he'll be slowed down with a lame horse by now. I can tell when a horse is badly shod — and his sure was! Yep! You'll catch him in maybe five or six hours. He rode east – like a fool — towards War Lance's territory!"

"I'd better get after him quick in that case!" Johnny mounted his horse and reined it round so that it began to gallop eastwards. "Thanks, Slim!"

"Y'r welcome, Johnny."

The blacksmith watched as Johnny's broad-shouldered figure disappeared in the distance. Then he went back to his forge. His hammer clanged ringingly on hot steel as he began work again.

Knox's tracks were still clear and Johnny had no difficulty in following them. A few hours before sunset he came to the spot where the horse-dealer's own mount had thrown a shoe. Two hours later, with the sun casting a red glow across the barren plain, broken only by clumps of mesquite bushes and tall cactus which cast long shadows, Johnny found Carl Knox.

The dealer was sitting on a rock drinking deeply from a leather canteen of water. He whirled, fingers clawing for his gun, as Johnny cantered down the trail towards him.

"Who in tarnation are you — and what do you want?" Knox's gun was out and levelled at Johnny.

"Put that gun away, Knox, I've come to help you out of a pretty tight corner if you only knew it!"

The Remington .38 remained levelled at Johnny's heart and Knox's eyes narrowed. "How d'you know my monicker, *amigo?*" He spoke thickly, his head cocked on one side questioningly. "And I'm doin' all right without your help — my horse cast a shoe, that's all!"

"Knox — it ain't only your lame horse that brought me out here. You're comin' back to Merikville with me. I think you're the hombre who's been spreadin' typhus around this neck o' the woods. Also this is injun country — you won't have a chance out here with War Lance up in arms."

"I've been out here before and looked after myself. You can go to blazes, stranger. I'm sticking here!

"Go back to Merikville, Mr. Nosy — this hogleg says y're goin' back an' so do I!" Knox waved the gun menacingly. Johnny launched himself for Knox, straight from the saddle he dived, hand locking on the horse-dealer's wrist.

The two men struggled desperately, Knox striving to bring the gun to bear on Johnny. But the young cowpuncher's iron-hard muscles were too much for the dealer. He gasped in pain as his hand was forced further and further back. With his right hand bunched into a tight fist, Johnny drove a long haymaker at Knox's jaw. With a soft moan, the man dropped to the ground and lay still.

"Sure am sorry I had to do that, pardner — but I don't like havin' guns pointed at me — an' you've got to see the Doc for the good of an awful lot of folks around here."

But Knox made no answer. He couldn't. He was out cold.

"Seems funny that a hoss-dealer should be so forgetful as to allow his hoss to cast a shoe," mused Johnny as he hefted the inert body of Knox over the saddle of his own horse. "An' this hombre seemed mighty anxious not to go back to Merikville. Still, I got to take him whether he likes it or not. If I'm lucky, I'll miss War Lance — if I ain't lucky — we've both had it!"

Night had fallen as Johnny began to lead his horse back towards the town. The coyotes were howling a sad song to the big moon which hung overhead, casting a strong light over the plains. Johnny wished that it wasn't so bright.

He was still wishing for clouds to obscure the moon when five Apache braves rose silently out of the rocks and stood menacing him with their rifles.

War Lance's Threat

Johnny said in the Apache tongue: "What do Apaches want with me? It is against their religion to make war at night."

One of the Apaches moved softly towards him, rifle pointed at his stomach. "You come with us, paleface. Chief War Lance want to ask you questions."

* * *

"War Lance — this man Knox is dangerous to your people! He brings disease with him. Look at your braves now —" Johnny pointed to where Apache braves were rifling his and Knox's saddle-bags, stuffing both white men's provisions into their mouths greedily. "You've got to let me take him back to the paleface camp!"

"No! I know you, He-who-rides-alone. I know you for a brave warrior and one who speaks true. But my people are at war with yours. In the camp named Shining Sands are three of my brothers. We trade. Your lives for my braves." War Lance was an old man but he still bore himself proudly.

"War Lance — this strife between our peoples is senseless. Why don't you return to your lands and leave us in peace?" Johnny was hopelessly trying to argue with the chief, but he knew that it was useless to try and talk to War Lance in the mood he was in.

War Lance said, "We kept our word — remained at peace with the paleface. But paleface comes and steals Apache horses. We ride war-trail for revenge."

"Okay, War Lance — have it your way. But I warned you!"

"You stay here until my braves are set free." That was the chief's last word. He gave orders for Johnny and Knox to be kept prisoner in a wickiup and strode away.

The Challenge!

In the wickiup, the wattle hut which the Apaches favoured as living quarters, Knox had woken up. He rubbed his jaw ruefully.

"Now look at the mess you've got us in!" he growled.

"You'd have been in this mess without my help." Johnny scratched patterns in the dusty floor with an old arrow shaft. "If typhus breaks out in this camp soon — I'll know for sure that you're the carrier."

"Aw — we'll both be dead by then."

"Maybe. But if I know Sheriff Bart Dawson, he'll take as long as he can haggling over details to give us a chance to escape if we can. It's a case of wait and see, Knox. And I've got a notion my hunch is goin' to be right."

Two days later almost the entire Apache camp was stricken by typhoid fever and Johnny knew beyond a shadow of doubt that Knox was the carrier. But now Johnny had two problems — to get out of the fix he was in and help the unfortunate Apaches who lay groaning in their primitive houses, tended by a shaman, or medicine man, who knew no way to cure them but that of invoking spirits to drive the devils of fever away. So Johnny asked to see the chief.

In War Lance's wickiup, the chief and his shaman sat waiting for Johnny to speak.

"War Lance — the magic of your shaman is doubtless strong for many things. But the paleface magic can cure your braves in no time. Let me ride to Shining Sands and bring back our doctor to cure your people."

"No!" It was the medicine man. "My magic is stronger. If you can prove otherwise, then you may bring your medicine man to try and cure the braves!"

Johnny had no choice. The medicine man had issued a challenge and he met it the only way he knew how. "Very well," he said, "We'll have a shootin' match. You can put a charm on the rifle of your best marksman and a curse on my rifle. I'll try to lift the charm and beat your marksman."

The shaman grinned triumphantly. "The victory of my magic is already won!" he said.

* * *

Those of the Apache tribe who could still walk stood silently watching the scene in the centre of the village. Johnny stood beside the medicine man and Fleet Wolf, the Apache's best marksman while the shaman went through a complicated ceremony, blessing Fleet Wolf's rifle and cursing Lonesome's.

"Oh, Great Spirits of the Earth and Sky! Put an eye into Fleet Wolf's rifle so that it may shoot straight and true. Put blindness into the bullets and rifle of the white man so that they will miss even a wikeyup at ten paces!"

"That seems pretty potent to me, shaman," grinned Johnny, appearing more confident that he felt, "What do we shoot at?"

"An arrow will be shot into the air. You will fire at it and hit it."

129

The chief raised his hand and Johnny and Fleet Wolf stood side by side, rifles raised, ready to begin. "Fleet Wolf will fire first." The chief stood back and dropped his hand.

An arrow, shot from a nearby brave's bow, sailed into the air and curved in an arc. Fleet Wolf's rifle cracked out once and the arrow split in two, falling to the ground. The Apache turned smiling. "Do better than that, He-who-rides-alone, and you will be more than a great shaman — you will be a great marksman."

Another arrow went flying skywards. Johnny tensed and took aim. *Bang!* The arrow split cleanly. *Bang!* One half split into quarters. A murmur of wonder went around the assembled braves.

"Is that good enough, chief?" Johnny turned to War Lance.

"It is good enough." The chief allowed no expression to cross his proud old face. "You will remain here as a hostage. The man named Knox will ride to Shining Sands for your medicine man."

Johnny shrugged. He couldn't ask for more even though he would have preferred to have gone himself. He only hoped Knox could be trusted.

In the wickiup he told Knox where to find Doc Weir and what to say to him.

"Right you are, Lonesome. Depend on me. Adios, amigo!"

Knox ducked his head and went out of the hut, making for the horse which the Apaches held ready for him. He mounted the steed and waved once to Johnny before he disappeared from sight, riding hard.

* * *

"We found him riding east," said the brave simply.

Johnny looked at Knox scornfully. "You dirty lowdown rattlesnake! You had no intention of going to Shining Sands. You were only interested in saving your own no-good scalp! I guess you'll be happy to know that you've probably caused the deaths of goodness knows how many white-men and injuns!"

Knox looked frightened. But he said in English so that the Apaches would not understand him: "Now see here, Lonesome, I've *got* to get away. It was me who stole those horses from the injuns. I sold 'em to Wade in Merikville. If you help me get away I'll give you two-hundred dollars — in silver!"

Johnny could hardly express his disgust. "So it was you who started this whole uprising! By thunder I ought to..." He barely controlled his anger. "I don't want your money, Knox. But I'll swear this — if we ever get back to town I'm going to see you get put behind bars for life!"

* * *

That night Johnny wondered desperately how he could escape from the Apache camp. Then he struck on an idea. If it worked — he might have a chance.

As Knox lay sleeping, Johnny began to groan and thrash about.

Soon the Apache guard heard him and came running in. "What is wrong, paleface? Have you caught the fever also?" He dropped his rifle and bent down to examine Lonesome. That was his mistake.

Strong hands shot up and caught the Apache about the throat, stifling any cries for help. The Apache was tough and as quick as an eel. With a grunt he broke Johnny's grasp and reached for a knife at his belt. Johnny grasped his knife-hand and brought in a left to the Indian's body. The Apache jack-knifed, his lungs striving to take in air, and Johnny knocked him cold.

Binding the Apache securely he took the man's rifle and walked cautiously out of the wickiup. "So-long, Injun," he whispered as he left. "I'll be back in time to help your people. I give my word on that."

131

He crept stealthily to the pony enclosure and mounted his own horse. He had no time to saddle it. Then he was off, riding like the wind for Shining Sands!

"Cure — or Kill!"

The doctor, still drowsy from his sudden awakening, rode beside Johnny as dawn broke over the hills.

"The Apaches may kill Knox if I'm not back soon." Johnny pushed his horse to even greater speed. "That I wouldn't care too much about — if the epidemic spreads to more tribes it's going to sure wreak havoc!"

"Then let's git movin', son. There ain't any time to lose!" The doctor's bag bumped against the side of his horse.

The mountains got nearer and within the hour they were standing before War Lance.

"Paleface, you are a man of your word and you have kept it, unlike your brother who lies tied in yonder wickiup. But if you and your medicine man do not cure braves — *you die!*"

"I think I can cure them all, given time," said Doc Weir opening his bag and taking out a precious packet of serum.

"Let's hope so, Doc," said Johnny, " 'Cause there ain't no cure for lifted scalp!"

But slowly and surely over the days, the Doc's care, his knowledge and the supply of serum began to benefit the sick Apaches. Within a week the whole tribe was on the road to recovery and Johnny, Doc Weir and the bound Carl Knox made ready to leave. The smiling chief gripped Johnny's hand.

"Your words have been proven true, He-who-rides-alone. From this day on I shall think more deeply before I act. There need never again be war between our people."

"I sure hope so, War Lance," replied Johnny. "And as for your horses, I'll see that Luke Wade gets his money back and the horses are returned to you. This skunk," he indicated the scowling Knox, "will get a life sentence on my evidence — it will keep him from stealin' other folks' property — an' keep him in quarantine so that he doesn't go spreadin' sickness around any more."

"Thank you," said the chief, "You will always be welcome in the villages of the Apache."

Adios!

"Well, Johnny, you cleared up a pretty big problem single-handed almost." Sheriff Bart leaned back in his chair, rolling himself a cigarette.

Johnny looked beyond his friend to where a disgruntled Knox had replaced the three Indians who had previously occupied the jail.

"Well," he drawled, "Mebbe that rattlesnake, Knox, actually did some good by spreadin' the fever. In fact — he more or less got himself arrested! If he hadn't been a typhus carrier no-one would ever be the wiser that he had stolen the horses. And War Lance would still be out raiding the homesteads, wagons and stage-coaches."

Bart said carefully: "Johnny — I've asked you this before — but would you care to take a job here? I need a deputy an'..."

"Sorry, Bart. I'm a drifter — guess I always will be. That's how I got my second name — Lonesome — I never had no other. I'll just roll along like the tumbleweed until I get good an' ready to settle down. Then maybe one day I'll come back and take that job."

Johnny picked up his hat from the sheriff's desk and shook his friend's hand. "Adios, Bart. I'll be moseyin' on down to New Mexico for a spell. I heard they need cowpunchers and are payin' pretty good money. I'll be back next summer maybe."

133

"Well, I hope there's some trouble on when you come back, Johnny," grinned the sheriff. "We'll need you around then."

Johnny grinned back and Bart followed him out of the door on to the sidewalk. The young puncher swung himself lazily on to his horse.

"Adios!" he said again as he rode out of town.

BRYAN TALBOT'S
THE ADVENTURES OF
LUTHER ARKWRIGHT

THERE'S SOMETHING SOLID and Northern English about a name like Arkwright. It suggests a man with his feet on the ground, prepared to look facts in the face and to do something about them if he has to. Luther, on the other hand, suggests a foreign quality, even an exotic, slightly visionary tinge which would once have been a little disturbing to the average inhabitant of the Lancashire mill-towns.

Nowadays, of course, those old weaving towns, which gave the Northern industrial landscape its character, no longer have the same stereotypical image. Beshawled and beclogged, shuffling at dawn over the hard cobbles to the factory gates, the workers were the epitome of ground-down wage-slaves. They took the brunt of the 'Hungry Thirties'.

Nowadays, when they have jobs at all, the workers are much more exotic. They may well still be the epitome of wage-slavery, but they wear saris and turbans and many speak Bengali as their first language. Even Mr. Grindem the Mill-Owner is probably now called Mrs. Patel. The average inhabitant of the mill-towns is as likely to worship at a mosque or a Hindu temple and still think of the Indian sub-continent as the motherland. The British Empire, in miniature, came home. Britain went from being the hub of the largest and most widespread imperium the world had ever known to a small, crowded nation that had become, almost overnight, multi-ethnic. It was a bit of a shock to the average native.

The conscious and often principled dismantling of the Empire which happened rapidly after 1946, with the coming to parliament of the first great socialist government, was accompanied by a shortage of man-power caused by the Second World War. Citizens of the British Commonwealth, mostly from the West and East Indies, were encouraged to emigrate to the United Kingdom to fill the thousands of jobs — most of them low-paid — which were urgently available.

After South Africa left the Commonwealth over the issue of apartheid, many South Africans also arrived, together with Nigerians and Ghanians. Frequently idealistic about the 'mother country', they found prejudice, wretched exploitation, poverty and a climate which, if you weren't born to it, can suck the soul from your eyes.

The absorption of these new cultures into the host culture was not as dramatic as some predicted (Enoch Powell, the 'intellectual fascist' of the Tory Party warned that racial conflict would bring 'rivers of blood' to Britain) and from the beginning there were people dedicated to the cause of social justice who, myself amongst them, eventually saw some of their idealism formalised in the Race Relations Act which made active prejudice, racial slurs and the like, illegal.

Alone, no such act ever changes society, and it did nothing to convince the skinheads and crypto-Nazis, but it does set the standard to which that society aspires. It said that the active expression of racial prejudice is unacceptable in a civilised world. Framed when memories of the Goebbels years were much fresher, the act certainly had respect for words and pictures. It admitted that they could kill.

In England, it did not stop the sentiently-challenged from abusing and attacking Pakistani women and children or beating up old black men or kicking a boy to death, but it did give the victims some means of restitution and it told them that they had specific recourse to the law. Of course it didn't stop racist policemen ignoring complaints (or indeed compounding them!), it didn't stop real life, with all its shades and variations, happening. It didn't stop many people being humiliated, insulted and attacked. But it did set a standard. A goal.

Britain needed goals. She needed, in fact, a whole new future. As she tried to re-invent herself from her self-image as the burdened mother of a thousand lands to become the European nation she had never accepted she was, many other social upheavals occurred. The imperial ghosts continued to haunt her. The problem of Ireland, whose Protestant population wished to remain within the United Kingdom and whose Catholics did not, was acerbated, originally by 'Reverend' Paisley, the Unionist adventurer. The Falklands folly, which need never have been resolved in violence and cheap flag-waving, seemed to say it all. If ever two politicians were deeply grateful for the chance to go to war and make cheap capital of human life, Margaret Thatcher and George Bush were. Now one goes raving mad and travels about America pretending to be the Queen, while the other looks enviously at his predecessor who stands a strong chance, in the trials of history, of getting off on medical grounds. But one thing's certain, they'll always have the blood of the dead on their hands. The ambitions of these greedy brutes permeate the pages of *Luther Arkwright*. His quests are quests for alternatives, for a better way.

In those golden years, which were not really an illusion, before the rich organised their attack on us, general prosperity increased significantly and, for a while, so did civic power (the poor were getting richer and the rich were not quite so rich as they had been). By the mid-1960s Britain was 'swinging' as far as the international community was concerned and the extraordinary vital mix of cultures had made the country probably the most creatively productive in the world. Ireland, as well as African America and Lancashire, gave us The Beatles and all the other extraordinarily talented musicians who changed the aspirations and capacities of popular music forever. All the arts thrived.

The spread of wealth resulted in a consequent spread of social justice. Macmillan's Tory party neither dared to nor cared to dismantle the social programmes introduced by their predecessors and when Labour was re-elected in the 1960s further enlightened legislation gave us for a while probably the best universally available health and education systems, free recourse to the legal system and much else. Although there was still a lot to fix, and we were beginning to understand the drawbacks of *any* orthodoxy, liberal or otherwise, it looked like we were getting to Utopia in the fast lane. We began to discuss what we were all going to do with so much leisure and wealth and equity...

Thatcher and Reagan represented very different interests to ours. They were in some ways the figureheads, following the direction of Big Business, who offered rhetorical legitimacy for an extraordinary grab-back of power by private capital from the public. They'd been planning it for years. I used to hear them, when I worked in Fleet Street in the early 1960s, talking about 'expanding into the public sector'. The old edicts of our common law — that that which concerns all, shall be determined by all — were ignored, even mocked. This powerful minority, which owned most of everything already, had no respect for us. The public institutions and utilities, designed to create a fairer society, were their chief targets. They corrupted the rhetoric of public debate, they claimed publicly-owned services didn't 'work' — i.e. they provided a service, not a profit.

Representing the interests of big business and preaching a free market philosophy of wild deregulation even crazier than the communism it sought to 'defeat' — a universal panacea somehow based on total internal competition which made a nightmare of most ordinary lives — they gave us a set of old-fashioned shoddy 'solutions' which got their friends and clients very rich indeed and the rest of us quite a bit poorer. They made virtues of greed and disharmony. The lie became a standard instrument of social intercourse, in government, in business and, eventually, throughout society. It also inevitably introduced uncertainties and miseries into our world which soon translated into violence and cynicism, eroded the quality of life of millions and continues to destroy it to this day. It was quite a radical change — more so in Britain, perhaps, than in America — and it was quite a lot for the average thinking person to cope with.

In the face of all this rapidly-gained experience and change, just on the cusp of the radical shift when we stopped being a community of citizens and instead were encouraged to become a loose confederation of independent consumers, creative artists were having a hard time.

The British cultural explosion which was first exemplified by the phenomenal success of The Beatles and other rock bands, as well as movies, comics and literature, occurred as a result of all these various experiences and social tensions. Faced with turning their experience and concerns into concrete work, many talented creative people looked to the conventional forms — the legitimate, respectable forms — and found them incapable of describing these daily realities. Indeed, if you tried to use them, they tended to distort what you needed to say. I had earned the large part of my living writing commercial comics in the 50s and early 60s and the techniques I had learned were very useful to me when I came to start writing the Jerry Cornelius stories, my first real attempt to match my writing to my observations and experience of my own world — the rapidly changing world of the 60s, the early years of the computer age. I was trying to describe, if you like, a 'post-modern' as well as a post-war world, using techniques which somehow achieved that better than more orthodox writing. Most science fiction and popular music of the time was crap, but it did offer us very useful methods and images.

Much of the talent which in an earlier world would have gone into conventional forms was now seeking better ways of expressing itself. The first 'pop' artists — Paolozzi and Hamilton in England, Kitai, Warhol and Co in the US — drew on comics and science fiction for their images and for a while gave a certain intellectual respectability to those genres. But in a way this was still the response of 'high' artists desperate for subject matter, something to rejuvenate the existing forms. The people who in my view were making genuine innovations were doing it mostly unrecognised and unheralded by the establishment (almost a credential) and they were doing it within the culture.

Out of this general movement, which gave us a vast range of different expressions, came *New Worlds*, the magazine I edited, together with the so-called sf New Wave when people like Ballard, Ellison and Sladek started throwing some effective literary hand-grenades about. In England this movement coincided and married with the experimental rock music movement as well as movements in poetry, painting and film-making.

From this same vibrant mix surfaced the new comic writers and artists like Alan Moore, Neil Gaiman and Bryan Talbot, inspired by the dynamics of American comics exemplified by the likes of Jack Kirby and Stan Lee, by earlier artists like Mac Raboy and Bob Kane, by the high standards of people like Frank Hampson, Don Lawrence and the Embleton brothers, by the products of the infamous and legendary Mick Anglo studio (which I had worked with) and by the new sf. They had the same impatience with genre as the 'New Wave' sf writers. They wanted the form to do more. They wanted it to say something. They wanted it to *express their experience.*

Amongst all this fine and impatient talent, Bryan Talbot soon began to stand out. By the late 1970's he had established a reputation as an original story-teller — one of a handful of graphic artists (Moebius, Chaykin and Simonson are others) who can tell a tale as well as they can draw one. He was marked by the ambition of his stories, as well as their skill. Here was something far more original and idiosyncratic than anyone had attempted before — essentially a way of describing not only what was happening to England, but also to the larger world, whose problems the UK frequently mirrored. An alternative history of modern times. And, of course, because Talbot was using a popular form to do this, it was also a very good, romantic, inventive, fast-paced yarn.

The pop-artists who had borrowed so much from comics and sf a few years earlier were still essentially taking surface elements, isolating them and introducing them into what was often highly academic art (Warhol is a good example) in some ways similar to the decadent academic art of 19th century France, where ideas of aesthetics and *refinements* of those aesthetics become more important and often more interesting than the subject.

Popular artists, on the other hand, are not allowed such luxuries. Substance, story and astonishment are what the audience demands.

It can't be talked into buying what it doesn't like. Your living doesn't depend on convincing an establishment that you are worth millions at auction. It depends on entertaining an audience — and keeping it entertained. The popular artist is called upon to master fundamental techniques which the pop-artist might imitate but rarely understands (in terms of their real narrative function, for instance). Narrative is very important in comics. In fact dynamics of all kinds have to be considered, as well as aesthetics. The superb black and white pages of Dudley Watkins, for instance, which are masterpieces of counter-balance and clever, unostentatious, internal design, almost certainly borrowing from Beardsley and the Robinsons, inspired many British artists, as did the classically good drawing and meticulous colour-work of Hampson, Lawrence, and Ron and Gerry Embleton (all of whom I was privileged to work with). In a graphic illustrator aesthetics are the hidden bones, sinew and life-stuff of the drawing, rarely advertised and never the subject. What is more, a kind of social consciousness frequently prevails in the work of the ambitious popular artist, perhaps in the tradition of Gilray and Hogarth, whose very directness of approach can make a very effective attack on the *status quo* and its evils.

Where this goes wrong is when the graphic artists become successful and self-indulgent, demanding that the public enjoy their skills rather than the story. We have all seen the unfortunate results. Other writer/artists have the good instincts and sense to make greater self-demands and teach themselves new techniques which *rise* to that ambition, so they are always trying — always straining for something extra — and it is this which gives their work at least part of its vitality. This is what is great about Talbot and it explains his steadily growing reputation. He clearly follows the Stephen King maxim that if you have the good fortune to be successful at something, it is your *duty* to try to get better and widen your ambition, to improve the climate for everyone.

I think Luther Arkwright — a kind of alternate history of the British Empire and its ongoing effects — improves all the time. He remains one of my own personal favourites and one of the best examples of what a talented writer/artist can do with a form. I believe that the reason the story remains so fresh and interesting is because, under all the glorious invention and wild adventure, glamorous characters and exotic machinery, Talbot deals in fundamental realities and makes stern self-demands.

He is *interested* in reality. He is *curious* about reality. He isn't, thank God, *afraid* of reality. His dialogue with the real world continues. His attempts to frame and communicate his real experience become increasingly complex and sophisticated. Certain proof of this came with the publication of *The Tale of One Bad Rat,* an admirably original use of the medium and one of the most coherent graphic novels ever published, which demonstrated not only how far Talbot had come from his early successes, but how far the genre itself could be taken.

There is nothing light or academic about the subjects Talbot is prepared to tackle! His taste for reality is as strong as his talent for fantasy. He comes from an area of England which, while often wild and beautiful, has a longer history of industrial exploitation and mass poverty than of widespread wealth and he witnessed the unpleasant results of the loony Right's appalling, self-serving financial and social policies. But he is neither pessimistic nor especially cynical. His visionary instincts tell him of a better world, perhaps a slightly more exotic world, which we might even achieve one day. Rather as Luther Arkwright's name suggests to me — his Northern feet are firmly on the ground but his visionary head is firmly up there peering around, reporting from the clouds.

And what great reports they are! I'm looking forward to the next Luther Arkwright. It gets better all the time. And so does Bryan Talbot.

Enjoy this wonderful story however you choose. There are plenty of levels you can experience it on. I know you'll get at least as much out of it as I do. If you're reading it for the first time, I envy you!

Michael Moorcock
Port Sabatini, Texas,
January 1997

DISARMING EVIL
A Review of From The Teeth Of Angels
Jonathan Carroll
HarperCollins, £14.95

J ONATHAN CARROLL'S BOOKS are dangerous. He takes considerable risks and trusts his readers with the nerve and intelligence to follow him. He's a moral visionary whose sturdy, subtle plots are rooted in character, a profound liking for people, a relish for life. Yet he writes about active evil. He uses supernatural fiction to comment upon itself, turn it on its head, bring it back to its roots in Revelations, in Bunyan, Milton, Blake and the great nineteenth century Romantics.

The appalling tensions of his narratives are as quietly achieved and as dreadfully effective as Elizabeth Bowen's in *Death of the Heart* or Angus Wilson's in *Late Call.* With Wilson, he shares an urgent concern for the fate of the world, for the consequences of lazy tolerance or careless liberalism.

For the past seven years, Carroll has produced a set of six novels about the same characters. The critic John Clute has called it the "Answered Prayers" sequence, for Carroll's people are frequently granted their heart's desire only to discover soul-threatening snags. The sequence began with *Bones of the Moon* which was followed by the increasingly sophisticated *Sleeping in Flame, A Child Across the Sky* and *Outside the Dog Museum. After Silence,* the penultimate book, only seemed to have supernatural elements. In reality, it was a painful, muscular examination of the moral consequences of avoiding truth, of failing to ask the right questions — of conspiring, if you like, with darkness.

Carroll comes from a background many would envy. His father a successful screen-writer, his mother a famous Broadway actress, he's familiar with the international arts world and lives between Los Angeles and Vienna. He understands the modern world and its temptations. His characters are usually self-knowing, well-educated, frequently rich, liberal and talented. They are film-stars, directors, writers, artists — public personalities. They have the power to make choices most of us only dream about. They often have charm and uncommon luck.

Sometimes they fall in love with perfect partners. At other times they experience the miraculous. They make important decisions that affect the world. And at some point in their stories they find themselves face to face with the Prince of Lies, who as often as not has turned up to demand payment with interest.

Carroll's characters react to the supernatural — from wise-cracking bull terriers to visions of the Pit — as most of us might. But they are always stronger the less they deceive themselves. And *when* they deceive themselves, they're soon floundering on the brink of the abyss. It's Carroll's great strength that you can find yourself approving the crucially wrong, sometimes cruel decisions that his complex, usually likeable, characters make.

As a deeply satisfying resolution and coda to the sequence, as well as a gripping independent novel, *The Teeth of Angels* describes how three very different characters — a boring English travel agent, a world-famous film actress seeking anonymity and a dying TV kiddy-show host — battle with death and the devil. Recalling the same sense of dread as *Brighton Rock*, Carroll details not so much the death of the heart as a calculated assault upon it. The most terrifying moment involves no supernatural elements at all, when one character decides to sleep with another who is HIV positive . . .

At this point we come to realise we have been experiencing a struggle between good and evil as monumental as anything in Milton (with whom Carroll shares an ability to make evil seductively beautiful and intelligent). In the end, good — or common humanity, as Carroll sees it — just about survives to fight another round due to a brave act of confrontation. "With all the power you have and all the fear you put in us, there's really only one thing you can do and that's scare us. You have your infinity of ways to do it, but *that's all.* I remember reading that Lucifer fell from Heaven not because he challenged God, but because God told him to worship man and he wouldn't."

Sometimes Carroll's own courage is unbearable, and we don't want to consider what he reveals. It's his extraordinary gift to trick us into confronting the stark truth of his revelations and keep us reading, terrified and illuminated, to see where we may have made our private compact with darkness. After all he has put us through, we continue to share his knowing idealism, his honest faith in the ability of the human spirit to redeem itself, to regenerate itself, and to triumph.

SIR MILK-AND-BLOOD

An Incident in the Life
of the Eternal Champion

WHAT'S THE TIME," he says. "Pad — what's the time? My watch has stopped."

"Four-thirty," says Patrick. "Shouldn't he have turned up by now?"

"He's always on time. He'll be here. God knows I'll be glad to get the release." He reaches for his cup. "It's bothering me, Pad. I can't get rid of it."

"You're bound to feel bad. After all, your brother —"

"Yes. But it's the kids, see..."

"There are no 'innocent victims' in a war," says Patrick. "Not in this war, anyway. You always reminded me how many of our children died to make them rich."

149

"Pad, I don't ever want to do that again. I didn't join to kill kids." As he looked at his companion's frowning face he knew he was saying too much. Even if you thought it, you never said it.

"Well, it's not likely either of us will have to do it again," says Patrick, ignoring this breach of etiquette. "In a little while we'll have our new passports and can be out of here. Anywhere we like, so long as it's not Ireland or the U.K. We can go to America. You've got relatives there, haven't you?"

"They read the papers," he says. But, anyway, he thinks, he won't be free there. He's ashamed to see his family. He already knows what they think of him. There isn't a news channel in the world hasn't shown the pictures of the ruptured tram, the children's bodies thrown everywhere, the weeping mothers. And his and Patrick's unshaven faces staring crazily out at them, their eyes reflecting the harsh flash of the camera. "By God, Pad, don't you wish you'd never got into this?"

"I don't think like that," says Patrick. "Since I was thirteen all I've ever done is this. I mean what else is there? What would you be doing now, if you hadn't joined the movement?"

"I was going to be a schoolteacher, God help me, before I got into politics." He lights a Gitane and goes to stare through the streaked grey window at the rain falling into the filthy water of the canal basin far below, where all six of the city's great underground waterways emerged into daylight and met at the infamous Quai D'Hiver. "I thought I could do more good in the movement."

As soon as he and Patrick were identified as the surviving bombers and their photographs had been published, they left London and travelled all the way to Paris from the Hook of Holland on a barge. It had taken a couple of weeks, but after a fortnight the authorities assumed they were far away from Europe. As it promised, the movement looked after them. Now their orders are to stay put until their 'release' comes. They have been told who to expect. When he arrives, there will be no mistaking him.

"I just wish it hadn't happened," he says.

"Jesus, don't you think I wish that, too! But it wasn't your fault. It wasn't my fault. And your bloody brother died a hero's death. It's him you should be grieving for. You think too bloody much. You have to put it behind you. Now, stop moaning on, will you? Honestly, it's really not cool to start up like this." Patrick seemed to regret the harshness of his tone. "You know that as well as I do."

He knows he's condemned to silence for the rest of his life. Once you join the movement, you never retire. You're 'released from active service' and that means the movement looks after you until it needs you again. He has never before longed with such passion to be free of it all.

"Well, look at it this way, we got a bit of collateral. That thing will make it easier for us, eh?" Patrick goes to the table and hefts the heavy newspaper parcel.

They had just left the tram at Waterloo Bridge. Tony was going on a stop or two, would leave his bag under his seat and then get the train at Charing Cross. When the bomb went off they had both been thrown flat by the blast and as they got to their feet, trying to catch their breath back, it was as if they had had a vision. The glass of the silversmith's was blown out and all the stuff in the window had been flung everywhere, apart from the one heavy object that had been central to the display and hadn't shifted or been damaged. An instinct developed from a lifetime of looting moved Patrick to grab the thing and then run for it. When they met up later, they discovered that Tony, sitting downstairs at the front of the tram, still had the bomb on his lap when it went off.

"Have another bloody drink, man." Patrick pours whisky into two glasses. "Go on."

"It doesn't work for me."

"God, you're a bloody morbid bugger! You're bound and determined, aren't you?" Patrick drains his own glass and takes the other. "It's a waste of time! Put it behind you, mate." He moves about the little room with impatient, aimless steps, as if his body tries to escape even as his brain tells him he has to stay. "This is guerilla warfare. Nobody wants the civilian casualties, but sometimes they happen. I don't have to remind you. You taught me. Was it our fault that the bomb went off too soon? If your stupid brother had set the bloody timer right none of us would be in this jam now!"

"Well, he's dead. And so are ten other people, mostly kids. Going home from the pictures on a Saturday night, looking forward to their tea."

"Oh, man, will you stop it! You're making it worse for yourself. Nobody was supposed to be hurt. The bomb should have gone off when the tram was in its shed. The sheds were supposed to be empty. The orders were clear. No casualties. Just do maximum damage to the turning plates. Our job's to disrupt travel and communications, not kill kids."

"But we did kill kids. And I can't get them out of my head. I can't stand the thought of another day of this! Oh, Jesus God, I want to be free of it, once and for all." Again he saw the disturbed disapproval on Patrick's face and fell silent.

"Well, you will be, any minute now." Patrick showed great self-restraint. "Who is this bloke? You know him, don't you?"

"He's a German, I think. I've been in the same company as him once or twice." He tried to keep his tone normal or at least controlled. "There was something odd about him. You can't tell how old he is. But he must be older than he looks. Mick says he was the youngest colonel in the SS." He sat back down in his chair, feeling a little better for talking. It took his mind off the bombed tram.

"After the war he went to South America and he was in Spain for a while and North Africa. He's been running guns for as long as I've been in the movement. And he's helped us with other stuff, of course. He was our main contact with Libya until that went sour. You could call him a soldier-of-fortune, a mercenary — I think he's nothing but a renegade. He has no loyalties at all. No cause, no religion and, as far as I can tell, no damned conscience."

"He sounds a superior sort of chap," says Patrick, emphasising his consonants the way they do in Kerry to announce sarcasm.

"Oh, he is, sure." He sighs. "No, I'm not kidding. There's something about him. When I was a kid, we used to have this story. It's one of those old Irish things, that seems to be just local." He puts out the Gitane and lights another. The room is misty with his smoke. "My granny used to tell it as 'Sir Milk-and-Blood' in English. She didn't speak much Gaelic, but I thought the name had to come from old Irish and I looked it up. I found something that sounded right in Cornish — *Malan-Bloyth*."

"You said he was German."

"My granny's story had him come from High Germany, which was probably Saxony, and finding the Holy Grail. But *Malan-Bloyth* wasn't a knight-errant seeking the Holy Grail, as he was in the *Sir Milk-and-Blood* version. His name means, as close as I can give it in English, *The Demon Wolf*..."

"For the love of God, what a bunch of crap," says Patrick, sitting down with a sigh on the corner of the iron bed. He looks about, as if for escape. "Holy Jesus, I could do with a cup of decent tea. Why the hell are you telling me a kid's story?"

"To pass the time. To take our minds off things. I was talking about this bloke."

"The German bloke?"

"My point is, he reminded me of the hero in my granny's story.

153

Red eyes, and very white skin. That was why he was called Sir Milk-and-Blood. He was a supernatural creature, a son of a Sidhe man and a human woman. In granny's version of the story, he was look-ing for the Holy Grail. In the other version, he's looking for the Magic Cauldron of Finn MacCool. You know..."

"I don't bloody know. I was never that interested."

"It's the sort of thing a patriot ought to know." He manages a smirk, to show he speaks in fun, but Patrick chooses to bridle anyway.

"Maybe. And maybe a patriot wouldn't keep going on about some poor bloody English kids he couldn't even know were on the damned tram." Patrick finishes his whisky and takes another Gauloise out of his pack. "So this is the bloke we're waiting for. What is he? A bloody werewolf?"

"Some believe that he was."

"I'm not talking about the fairy story. I'm talking about the real bloody bloke. What's he got? Leprosy?"

"Maybe. I first met him in the Med, off the coast of Morocco. He was with Captain Quelch, another damned renegade, on that boat that almost got blown out of the water off Cuba the other day — *The Hope Dempsey*. We were dealing with some kind of volatile cargo, nobody ever said what it was, but I could guess, of course. My job was to check the boxes and pay over the money. I was always a better quartermaster than I was a field soldier..."

"Tell me about it," says Patrick, glaring disgustedly into the rain. He hears a movement on the uncarpeted stair and rises from the bed.

The two men wait, but it's a false alarm.

"Well, he's a cold fish, by the sound of it," says Patrick. "What else do you know about him?"

"Not much. He's some sort of German prince, but everyone calls him 'Monsieur Zodiac'. He spent a lot of time in the Far Atlas, speaks their languages, does business with the Berbers. They say he has one of those big villas in Las Cascadas. But Donald Quinn told me he lives in Egypt most of the time."

"Why is he interested in that?" With his unlit cigarette Patrick indicated the newspaper parcel.

"It's his price. The movement arranged it."

"Well, let's hope he brings cash," says Patrick, scratching at his bottom and sighing. "I don't know about you, but I could do with some sunshine. Another few days and I'll be on a beach in Florida, soaking up the rays."

"What happened isn't that important to you, is it, Pad? You've already forgotten it."

"No point in doing anything else," says Patrick. "An incident in the ongoing struggle. You can't make it not have happened. A bad dream. Leave it behind, mate, or it'll fester forever. Or go and see a bloody priest and get it off your bloody chest. Jesus Holy Christ! You're no bloody fun any more. I'll be damned glad to see the back of you!" And he begins that agitated pacing again, so that neither of them hears the soft knock. A second knock and Patrick is rushing for the door, dragging it wide.

"I told you he'd be on time."

And there he is. He would be a little less terrifying if he wasn't smiling.

"Well, thank God, at bloody last!" says Patrick, studying the tall stranger with nervous resolve.

Although it is only late afternoon, Monsieur Zodiac wears perfect evening dress. Thrown back over one shoulder is an old-fashioned scarlet-lined opera cape and on his head is a silk hat. His eyes are hidden by a pair of round, smoked glasses which further emphasise the pallor of his skin. He has a long head with delicate bones and his ears seem to taper. He has an almost feminine mouth, sensitive and firm. In one white-gloved, slender hand is an ebony cane, trimmed with silver. In the other, he carries what appears to be a long electric guitar case which he now stoops to rest on the floor.

"Good evening, gentlemen." He speaks in a soft accent that is difficult to identify. "Such confidence is flattering. I believe you have something to show me?"

Patrick backs into the room as Monsieur Zodiac carries in his burden, puts it down again, takes off his hat, closes the door carefully behind him and nods a greeting. Slipping a slender silver case from his inner pocket, he removes a small, brown cigarette and lights it. He comes immediately to the point. "I have your release, gentlemen. But first I must be sure that you are who you say you are and that your circumstances are as they have been described to me."

"What do we have to bloody prove?" says Patrick. "That we blew up a Number 37 tram in the Strand? The movement knows who we are. They sent you, didn't they?"

"Not exactly. I volunteered to come. I had heard about that —" he gestures with his cane at the parcel on the table. "And when I learned what I was to receive for my services, I put two and two together. So that was your bomb on the Number 37?"

"It was," says Patrick, dropping his cigarette to the boards of the floor and crushing it out. His companion is silent. Monsieur Zodiac removes his smoked glasses and lifts a pale, enquiring brow.

Patrick now takes note of the albino's ruby eyes which burn with suppressed pain and melancholy irony.

Caught for a moment in their timeless depths, Patrick feels suddenly lost, as if his entire universe has fallen away from him and he is absolutely alone. Gasping, he turns and almost runs towards the table, tearing at the newspaper. "You'd better have a look at this cup..."

"No," says Monsieur Zodiac. "I don't want to see it. Not quite yet. I know what it is, believe me. I'll wait. Until you're gone."

"So you trust us?" says Patrick. He looks expectantly towards the guitar case. He is very anxious to leave. His companion, however, sits quietly in his chair, and his nod to his old acquaintance has a reconciled, almost submissive air. He makes no effort to prepare himself for departure.

"To be who you say you are? Of course I do! Who else would claim such a crime?"

"Jesus God Almighty," says Patrick. "Crime is it? I can't stand another damned moralist. I'd be prepared to bet you've just as much blood on your hands as we have."

"Oh," says Monsieur Zodiac lifting the case onto the table. "Infinitely more, no doubt."

This confession of complicity, as he sees it, relaxes Patrick a little. He gestures to the bottle and glasses. "A drink, pal?"

The albino moves his head a fraction. No. His strange, almost angelic face turns to the window and notes that it is overlooked by nothing.

"You brought cash I see," says Patrick. "And travellers checks, like we asked, I hope?" He hesitates as the albino rapidly snaps open the case's catches and begins to lift the lid. There's a walkman or something in there, playing what sounds at first like modern North African music. The noise deepens until it vibrates all the glass in the room and makes Patrick feel faintly ill. Some sort of alarm, perhaps.

Then the case is fully open. It is lined in red velvet. The whole of its length and much of its breadth is taken up by an enormous broadsword. The thing is so impossibly ancient its iron has turned jet black. And along the length of the blade run a series of disturbing red runes which, even as he watches, seem to move and reshape themselves constantly, in unison with the strange, deep howling which springs from the trembling metal. In the hilt what looks like an enormous ruby pulses in harmony with the sword's unnerving voice.

157

"What the hell is that?" Patrick valiantly demands, trying to guess where the money's hidden.

The albino seems amused. For a moment, he has a panting, wolfish air to him as he reaches both hands towards the case.

Somehow the black sword, almost as tall as he is, settles into Zodiac's grasp, its voice changing to one of profound satisfaction as it unites with its master. It shudders as if with eager anticipation. Now, with a new calmness, Monsieur Zodiac turns towards the seated man, and there is still an element of compassion in his flaming red eyes.

The whole world fills with the sword's rising song. The runes race and whirl, forming and reforming to create whole new languages of power as they writhe up and down its black length. The universe trembles. The room fills with darkness. That same darkness floods out of the window and silences the Quai D'Hiver.

As Patrick begins to vomit uncontrollably, the albino smiles.

"It is your release," he says.

THE END